FIRE
BOMBER

The Shadow Club Series
Book One

by Russell Cederberg

Published by Lorien Ltd. 2018

For more information about the author, please visit:

www.rcederberg.com

FORWARD

The time frame of this story is the autumn of 1990. Although this does not seem like a really long time ago, things back then were *very* different. Home computers were in their infancy and very few households had access to one. Although mobile phones existed, they were also a brand new idea and were almost exclusively used for business. Email was mostly provided by a company called Compuserve. Public access to a brand new concept called "The Internet" was very limited and mostly ignored. Although digital cameras existed, the price was exorbitant and the quality was very low so any serious photographer still used film. It would take 13 years for the price to come down far enough and the quality to go up far enough for digital cameras to outsell film cameras. Most families had a tube-style TV set, 27 inches was considered large. They would also have had a VCR. Blockbuster video had been around for 5 years.

One of the motivations for me writing this story was to illustrate how much the paradigm of communication and relationship has changed since 1990. In our modern-day paradigm, it is assumed that communication is ubiquitous and instant and a photograph has almost no intrinsic value. In 1990, a long-distance phone call; any phone number outside of your immediate area, actually cost money. Photographs were fairly expensive and not altogether common and a letter was only a handwritten or hand-typed item you received in your actual mailbox. Kids would often spend some time talking on the phone, but most communication occurred face-to-face. It is in the context of this kind of social structure that this story takes place.

PROLOGUE

A solitary man stood in a dark alleyway in front of an empty warehouse building in downtown Portland. The street was deserted except for the first leaves of autumn that rattled down the dirty gutters in the chilly late night breeze. The surrounding buildings were all older and the entire neighborhood was run down. He had been there for a long time and was intently watching the warehouse across the street.

Suddenly, from inside the warehouse, there was a dull boom and a flash of orange flame from several of the windows, and the man gasped a quick and shallow breath of delight. Within 30 seconds every window in the place was lit by bright orange flames and the fire alarm went off with a brash clang. The man's breathing quickened and he began muttering to himself, pacing back and forth like a caged animal. A car drove by on the street and stopped and the people got out, chattering and pointing. A small crowd began to form from a nearby apartment building, attracted by the alarm.

The man stepped out of the shadows. His eyes shone bright and evil like the orange flames and a wicked smile split his face like a crack in the end of a burning log.

CHAPTER ONE

Seth Knight stood up from his lunch in the cafeteria of Taft High School and pushed the still half full lunch tray away with a scowl.

"Another day, another plate of slop. This cafeteria is weak," he muttered.

Seth stood and watched the people eating for a moment, his sky blue eyes glazed over with a smoldering fire that always signified deep thoughts. He ran his fingers through his thick, almost jet black hair, dug his fists into the small of his back and stretched backwards until his spine popped like a boxer's knuckles. Seth was tall, with a wiry 175 pound frame and square shoulders. He was mysteriously handsome with an infectious smile.

The huge, shabby young man who sat opposite him at the table looked longingly at Seth's lunch.

"Gee, Seth, can I have it?"

"Sure, Greg. Chow down."

Greg Francovich grasped the tray and dug into the food. Seth glanced around the cafeteria and noticed a clump of people gathering around a large plastic trash can at the other end so he walked over to have a look. Somebody had lit the trash can on fire, but the crowd was holding back, unsure of what to do.

Seth shook his head and sighed, then grabbed the nearby fire hose coiled on the wall.

"Scuse me! Pardon me! Hot coffee! Lady with a baby!" he yelled as he pushed his way through the crowd. As soon as he reached the can he pointed the hose at the flames that were melting the can and, with a huge grin on his face, proceeded to spray

3

not only the can but also the crowd. Gasps and yells filled the cafeteria as the crowd scattered, but then somebody started cheering for Seth and soon the whole crowd was cheering him on.

Suddenly a squeaky voice cut through the din and a skinny teacher in a dingy suit elbowed his way over to Seth.

"What, what do you think... who in the world, look! Look what you've done to my lunch, young man!" he finally managed to spit out.

He held the plate right up to Seth's nose and shook it. The plate contained the soggy remains of a hamburger smothered with raw onions.

Seth twisted his face into a grimace and he moaned, "You call that lunch!!? Smells like the locker room to me!" and the crowd erupted into laughter.

Seth realized that Mr. Billingsworth was really upset and raised his hands in a gesture to silence the crowd.

"Look, sir. I'm really sorry this happened, but someone lit the can on fire-"

"You will come with me right now to the office, young man. That over-spraying was most deliberat and-"

The crowd interrupted him with loud booing and several rude remarks, but Mr. Billingsworth just raised his voice.

"-And I for one think it's high time you students were taught how to respect your elders and..."

His voice was lost in the noise of the crowd, so he stopped talking and pointed towards the door.

Seth shrugged his shoulders and walked out with the irate teacher.

"Can't fight city hall," he muttered to himself.

~ ~ ~

Lake Oswego was a small town just south of Portland. It had a lovely lake right in the center of town, a quaint downtown section and Taft High School was small but had a reputation for excellence. Dwight Stone was the head counselor at Taft.

After having a pleasant lunch, Dwight whistled as he walked back to his office. He was looking forward to some relaxing paperwork that would keep him occupied for several hours. He was stopped short by four familiar faces waiting in the hall for Mr. Moore, the vice principal. Dwight caught the end of Seth's slick conversation with the new school receptionist.

"...Student? I'm flattered! I haven't heard that for a while. Actually, I'm a talent scout from Hollywood and I'm here to see Mr. Moore about recruiting some students for a movie. By the way, your eyes are remarkable, have you ever done any film work-"

A snore like a hovering helicopter destroyed Seth's smooth approach. Greg Francovich, Seth's lunch companion, was slumped in his chair, sound asleep, with his hands touching the ground and his size 14 work boots looking like small, up-ended trucks. Gunther Stern, Greg's best friend who was practically half his size burst out laughing with a loud squeal,

"Jeez Seth, smooth moves!"

Dwight noticed the fourth student, Travis West, sitting with his thick arms folded across his huge chest and his face expressionless.

"Hey Travis, great game last Friday! What are you doing here with these troublemakers?"

Travis turned away and mumbled, "Waiting to see Mr. Moore."

Dwight suddenly realized his plans for a quiet afternoon were spoiled, but he really didn't mind.

"What am I going to do with you guys?" he said, shaking his head in amazement.

"C'mon into my office."

Dwight's office usually looked as if he had just moved in, with books and papers stacked everywhere, and today was no exception. He leaned back in his chair and propped his feet on the desk.

"I think an appropriate course of action here today would be to remind you gentlemen about your histories here at Taft and exactly where you stand in this establishment."

With a surgeon's precision, he knifed through a pile of papers on the floor and extracted three red file folders.

"Gunther Stern." He flipped open the folder and withdrew a pile of pink slips.

"Let me see here. This one is from when you hacked security on the school district computer system, gained access to confidential files and crashed the system in the process, losing a whole week's worth of information-"

Gunther interrupted, "Wait a minute! One of their operators crashed it. I was doing a random, read-only seek on the database, but the sys-op was reorganizing the whole file, so I just laid back and waited 'til he finished. Next thing I know he transposes the hexadecimal address, and it just happened to be right where the supervisor code was loaded. It crashed so hard it must have smoked. I just sat there and watched."

Dwight fought back the smile that always tried to form on his face when he talked to Gunther. It was really hard to take language like that from a 13 year old kid even if he was a genius. Gunther was technically a child prodigy, and had skipped several grades in elementary school.

"I think the main issue here, Gunther, is you being where you shouldn't have been in the first place. And could this incident have had anything to do with the unlisted phone number of a certain rather buxom young lady named Gloria Bradey?"

"You can't prove that," he said, but the flush in his cheeks was all the proof necessary.

"Smooth moves!" Seth whispered with a grin.

"Moving right along, here we have the floating hydrogen-balloon-bomb caper at the football game,"

"That was you? I thought it was world war three with those things blowing up over the football field," Seth said with a big smile.

"The box of cockroaches you let loose in home economics..."

Gunther began to squirm.

"Laundry detergent in the faculty toilet. I mean really, Gunther, this is High School. How about the unsolved mystery of the fruit fly epidemic in Mr. Myrtle's science class? Could you have had anything to do with that one?"

There was a long pause. "So what are you in here for today Gunther?"

"Mr. Billingsworth was getting his dates mixed up again in Government and I was just trying to-"

"Just trying to help, but forgetting to be polite again. Correct?"

"Well, sometimes he gets so boring and-"

"You need to raise your hand and then wait for the teacher to call on you."

He reached for the next folder.

"Enough said. Now, Greg Francovich. Sleeping in class, asleep in class, eating in class, ah, here's one. Unacceptable personal hygiene; student needs to wear more appropriate clothing, ah, academic failure, GPA of 1.0, what was it today, Greg?"

"I sorta fell asleep."

"Let me see that pink slip you have, Greg. Disrupting class with loud snoring. Billingsworth's class again, huh? Sounds as if Billingsworth isn't having a very good day today. Greg, you need to try a lot harder. I really believe you can do much better than you are doing. I just don't know how to help you. I guess I need to get together with your folks again, right?"

"Okay, Dwight."

Dwight opened the last folder and withdrew a large pile of slips.

"Seth Knight. Hmmm. Rude and intolerable exhibitionism in the cafeteria with pie. No respect for the dignity of-"

"Oh, Dwight, what's wrong with a pie eating contest?"

"Okay, how about smoking in the boys locker room?"

"Hey, man, you know I don't smoke. We were, ah, you know... burning farts."

"That's disgusting, Seth."

He looked up from his folder with a twinkle in his eye.

"And can you imagine what would have happened if Mr. Moore had walked into that assembly at City High instead of me?"

"I heard something about that Dwight. What actually happened?" Gunther squeaked.

Seth spoke up quickly. "It was nothing. Never mind."

"Now, Dwight, we have a right to know. Wouldn't you agree?" Gunther insisted. Dwight leaned back and smiled.

"It was really unbelievable. He should have won an Oscar for that performance. Last month I was at City High School in Portland for a district counselor's meeting. During the lunch hour I attended an assembly with the rest of the student body to hear the readings of one Hasse Bjornsson, supposedly a famous Swedish poet/philosopher on a U.S. tour. Hasse Bjornsson was introduced, and lo and behold, Seth Knight walks on stage, dressed in a suit and false goatee and reads poetry for 30 minutes. They even gave him a standing ovation at the end. And where did you get all that poetry, Seth. I didn't recognize a line of it. At any rate, what's your excuse for today?"

"Well, I guess I had a run in with Billingsworth as well-"

"What were you doing in Government class? We all know you don't take any real classes."

Everybody laughed. Then Seth briefly told them about the incident in the cafeteria with the burning trash can.

"Well, I hope you actually sprayed most of the water on the fire. At any rate, I'm sure I can get you out of this one."

Dwight paused for a moment and stared hard at Travis.

"Now you, Travis, you're a different story altogether. What are you doing here?"

"I tackled coach Gazoni yesterday at football practice after school and threw him in the mud. He gave me this pink slip just a minute ago when I went to PE class."

They all stared at him in disbelief. A long minute of silence followed. Wasn't this the true blue coaches pet and star athlete with an almost military do-or-die attitude? The model student after whom all the colleges were clamoring? The one guy on the team who never had a bad word to say about coach Gazoni?

Dwight broke the silence.

"What happened?"

"Aw, he had me doing goal line tackle drills with Billy Weeks, and I was supposed to be going 100%. I could kill a guy that small, Dwight, and he made us do it over and over, Billy was crying...I just couldn't stand it any more."

Seth shook his head in amazement. "What a day to go home early. I wish I had a picture. What did he say anyway?"

"Billy and I just left after that, and I don't care what he says. What he was doing was wrong, and he knows it. Even my dad would back me on this one."

Dwight sat rubbing his chin for a moment.

"To tell you the truth, Travis, I'm not too worried about you right now. I'm sure Moore will hit the ceiling as usual, but when he calms down he'll probably just file it and forget it like he seems to do with a lot of things. It's you I'm worried about Seth. What I need to come up with is a way to get you off of Moore's hit list. I can't really understand why you are there to begin with, to tell you the truth. You really don't ever cause that much trouble..."

Kate, Dwight's secretary, walked in and interrupted.

"Here is a note from Mr. Moore about the school newspaper staff, Dwight. I think he still needs more people."

Dwight sprung out of his chair with the agility of a spider monkey and a smile split his face in two.

"Kate, you're an angel." He took the notice and turned around.

"This is perfect. It's just what we need. You are now a member of the Taft Chronicle staff, Seth."

"Now just a minute here, Dwight. I really don't think I need to go to that kind of extreme-"

"As a matter of fact, Seth, I believe that you do. Mr. Moore has been watching you like a hawk all year and is just waiting for a good excuse to send you home for a few days. A suspension would not only get you removed from the team, it would really hurt your father as well."

"But I don't know anybody on the paper and I really don't have any interest in..."

"Travis has been working for the Chronicle for over a month now."

Seth looked at Travis with mild surprise.

"Really man?"

"Sure. I enjoy it a lot. Gives me an excuse to use my camera more."

Dwight continued, "Both Greg and Gunther have been part of the paper for awhile now. I really don't know why I didn't think of it before. It's such a great idea. And if what I hear is true, you are rather gifted in writing. Working for the paper would give you an outlet for that talent. What do you think?"

"I don't know, Dwight..."

"Now, you've got to act all excited about it or it won't work. Do a good job and I'll guarantee you'll be left alone. How 'bout it?"

"Dwight, you're a weasel, you know that? I don't know anybody who can finagle the way you can-"

"Except for you, of course!" Seth said with a twinkle in his eye.

They all burst out laughing but their brief revere was abruptly murdered by the door swinging open. Mr. Moore came hulking in.

"What the hell is going on in here?!" he growled, his drill sergeant voice sounding like fingernails drawn across a chalkboard. Dwight reacted cool and professional. It was his job to mediate between his students and this man, and he did a fabulous job.

"Greg, go wash your face and get back to class. Please try a little harder today, and I'll have the conference with your father next week as planned. Gunther, I want you to raise your hand *every* time you want to speak in class. Now march, and meet me here after school. Travis, you'll have to wait in here while I speak with Mr. Moore privately. Seth, let's go have a word with Mr. Moore in his office."

He promptly marched out with an air of authority and Seth followed.

Mr. Moore looked around with scowl on his face. He knew something was being covered up, but then, it seemed like people were always trying to hide things from him.

"I'll get to the bottom of this one," he muttered as he swaggered into his office behind Seth.

CHAPTER TWO

Mr. Moore tried to regain control of the situation as he swung his office door closed.

"I've been informed that we had a problem in the cafeteria today and I think that it's time to take serious steps in dealing with-"

Dwight cut him off and ruined his speech.

"Yes, Bob, I completely agree with you."

Mr. Moore's jaw dropped. He had been expecting Dwight to try and stall Seth's punishment. Dwight continued.

"I think this trash can fire situation is getting out of control and I thought Seth's action today was totally commendable. You of course heard that the can was in the cafeteria-"

"Now hold on just a minute, Dwight! According to the report I received-"

"Yes, Bob, I'm sure in the excitement Mr. Billingsworth left out a few details. For example, the can was plastic, and we both know that burning plastic emits deadly poisonous fumes. This threat however, was completely averted by-"

"Dwight, I think you're looking at this situation-"

"Averted by the quick, and I might add, *heroic* reactions of Seth here. You naturally can picture the possible panic when students start to choke and get queasy from the invisible fumes-"

"I can hardly believe that one small trash can-"

"And then there is the obvious problem of damage. Melting, burning plastic on our new flooring in there, smoke damage to the acoustic tile ceiling, the possibility of the fire spreading, rising liability insurance rates, why, Seth probably saved the school thousands of dollars today, Bob, quite literally. I'm sure you can see my point."

Money always had a way of turning Mr. Moore's head around.

"Yes, I suppose you could look at it that way."

"Now, Bob, I think an appropriate course of action would be to have Ronald print an article in the next Chronicle about the fire situation, stressing how really childish it is, and capping it off with a report on Seth's heroics today. What do you think?"

Even Seth was amazed at Dwight's prowess when Mr. Moore begrudgingly agreed.

"Yes... I suppose that would be appropriate."

"Well, I've got Travis to attend to in my office. Good afternoon, Bob."

He glided out of the office, winking at Seth as he went by to remind him of their previous conversation. Seth took the cue and continued on where Dwight left off.

"Now that we're on the subject of the newspaper, Mr. Moore, I understand that you're a little short-handed, so I'd like to offer my services. Dwight was commenting on how I should be putting my writing abilities to work, and it got me to thinking. Do you suppose that would be all right, sir?"

He winced inside at having to call Mr. Moore 'sir'.

This turn of events ruined Mr. Moore's day, but he reluctantly agreed to let Seth work on the paper.

~~~

After school, Seth poked his head into Dwight's office. Dwight and Tina Beverly, Seth's English teacher, were having a chat.

"All right, what's going on in here? What kind of crap is Dr. Stone trying to pull on you today, Miss Beverly?" His eyes danced with mirth.

"Nobody pulls any, ah, anything on me, Mr. Knight, nobody." She couldn't hide her smile behind her boisterous words.

"How's the newspaper business, lizard lips?" Dwight countered with a twinkle in his eye.

They all laughed. Seth always wondered why more of the teachers at school couldn't be more like these two, so human. Many of the teachers elevated themselves far out of touch.

"Gone melancholy on us, Seth?" Dwight asked after a pause.

"No, I was just wondering why so many teachers around here have to act so superior all the time. It's like they've got something to prove. Like Billingsworth today. What a goon. You two are, well you're at least honest with me. You know what I mean?"

His sky blue laser eyes burned into Dwight and Tina for a moment, then he laughed, the mood passing.

"I swear, Dwight, I've never seen Mr. Moore so confused in my life. Did Dwight tell you what happened, Miss Beverly?"

She nodded an affirmation.

"I scored one of my own though. I think calling him sir was the clincher Dwight. I don't know. He agreed too fast. I bet this thing is going to backfire and I'm going to get stuck doing some dumb thing all year-"

"You've got to trust me there, Seth. I think you're going to be surprised at how this turns out, and I really think you will enjoy working with Travis, Greg and Gunther once you get to know them-"

"That's another thing, man. Why in the heck are you lumping me together with those three other guys? I've got nothing at all against Greg, but that Gunther kid is a weasel! I don't care if he is a genius. I don't know anyone besides the hard core jocks who will have anything to do with Travis either. I mean, I've played on the same team as him for three years and I don't think I've exchanged two sentences with him in my life. He hardly talks at all."

Dwight turned on Seth with fire in his eyes.

"Hold on just a minute, Seth! I happen to know Travis really well, and I don't care how much time you're on a team with someone. If you never talk to him, you can't know what he's all about, now can you? Travis is an intelligent, sensitive person; just really quiet, and really driven by his father. The freedom your father gives you is a luxury most people don't have, so I say give the guy a chance. You're always screaming about getting a fair chance yourself. Probably more than anyone I know. So practice what you preach. The same goes for the others, too. You guys have the potential to do something good around here, but it starts with you, Seth. You've got to be the leader and you've got to take the initiative."

By the time Dwight finished his speech, he had risen to his feet and was leaning across his desk, staring hard at Seth. Seth stood staring at his feet. It wasn't often that Dwight came down so hard on him.

He spoke slowly, "Well man, if it's got to be, it's got to be, I guess. I just wish I knew what I did to deserve Moore's attention this year Dwight."

With that, he spun around and whisked out of the room.

~ ~ ~

That afternoon, when most of the students had gone home for the day, one particularly skinny and ill-clad student stood lounging on the asphalt walkway next to the auditorium. He was smoking a cigarette all by himself. He stood and stared at the smoke as it rose in a thin line from his cigarette, studying it with a look of fascination on his face. He had been there for a long time. As he reached the end of his cigarette, a dirty smile flashed across his face and he reached into his pocket and withdrew a book of matches. He carefully tore one single match from the book and then replaced the book in his pocket. As he took one last drag from his cigarette, he touched the match head to the glowing end of the cigarette and his eyes lit up like jewels with the flare and flame of the match. With a quick puff of smoke from his thin lips, he tossed the lit match and cigarette butt together into the trash can next to him and hopped over the low hedge that was next to the asphalt walk, and then trotted down the street.

The tiny flame in the trash can quickly spread and soon it engulfed all of the trash in the can, sending flames and sooty smoke into the air. The skinny student paused in his retreat after about a block and looked back over his shoulder for a long, lingering look at his handiwork, then turned and disappeared over a low fence around someone's backyard.

CHAPTER THREE

Lake Oswego, a small but rather prosperous town just south of Portland, lay blanketed in a cold morning mist that drifted through the town's massive fir trees and hugged the surface of the lake, painted amber by the rising sun. Seth stood silently at the edge of the lake staring at the shimmering ground fog on his way to school. He was in no hurry to be on time to the school newspaper staff meeting.

The Taft Chronicle had a short staff meeting each morning at 7 AM. Mr. Moore had assigned his son Ronny to be the editor after Ronny had lost the election for Student Body President. With Ronny as the editor of the paper however, it was very difficult to keep people interested in staying involved. Five people had already quit the paper and this morning June Dunkinberger, the business manager, had left her casual resignation note taped to the door.

Ronny started the meeting with his usual roll call.

"Annie Bartholemew."

"Here."

"Cathy Doherty."

"Here."

"June Dunkinber– uh, Jann Paris"

"Here."

"Marla-"

Marla Wexler interrupted. "Ronald, I swear you'd call role if only one person showed up. I've lots of things that need looking after and I wish you'd get on with it. Now, why do you suppose June quit, Ronald, and what will we do now? I certainly can't do her job and my job as well and it's certain that nobody else here can do it. Are you going to get your dad to pull you out of this one too?" She was very outspoken, and it sometimes got her into trouble.

A squeaky voice rang out from the back of the classroom.

"Gee, where is everybody?"

Gunther walked in dragging Greg by the belt. Greg's hair was plastered to one side, and his shirt was hanging out. He obviously wasn't awake yet.

"What's this I hear about June quitting, and who's going to run the paper now?" Gunther said with a smile.

"As to who runs the paper, kid-"

"The name's Gunther. Not kid. Gunther!"

"Fine. Fine. Now it's the editor's job to run this paper, and since I am-"

"A figurehead!" Gunther's squeaky comment was accented by a loud burst of laughter from the back of the room as Seth walked in.

Ronny was perplexed. "What, ah, what are you doing here?" He tried to be as polite as possible.

Seth sat down, leaned forward, and looked Ronny right in the eyes.

"I work here now, pal. What's your excuse?"

Gunther snorted with a giggle and the rest of the staff tried their best to suppress their laughter. Ronny lost his temper momentarily and tried to restore some order to his staff meeting.

"Okay now guys, could we just cut out the cute humor and grow up? We've got a lot of catching up to do to finish this edition in a week, and I can't do it all by myself. Does anyone have any bright ideas? So far we have the story on Miss Skondberg's art show at the mall..."

Seth groaned. Sylvia Skondberg was Seth's idea of the most beautiful woman in the world. She also happened to be his art and drama teacher.

"...a behind-the-scenes look at the cafeteria, an article on horses by Cathy, some poetry from Miss Beverly's senior writing class, and all the usual columns."

"What about the story on the drama department Ronald?" Annie demanded.

"Oh sure, sure. I forgot about that."

"What about arson?" someone called from the back of the room. It was Travis.

"Sorry I'm late, Ron. Personally, I'd like to do an article about these stupid trash can fires. It's getting ridiculous around here. I was thinking about tying the story in with all the fires downtown lately. How 'bout it?"

"Well, uh, Travis, the arson story sounds real interesting, but we have to have our copy ready by Monday. You think you can do it that quick? I sure couldn't come up with-"

Travis cut him off. "No sweat!"

Ronnie sat with an open mouth for a minute.

"Oh. Well, if you want to run a photo with that we'll need it by Monday as well so George can drop it off at the print shop with the copy."

"I'll definitely have a photo for you Ron. No problem."

Ronny then looked over at Seth.

"So, ah, so what are you going to be doing with the paper, Seth?"

"To tell you the truth, man, I haven't figured it all out since your father asked me to help out last week, so why don't we just play it by ear for a while?"

Ronny wasn't about to argue with Seth, so he let it go at that.

"Well, with Travis' article on the fires and Annie's story on the drama department, I suppose we could squeeze by. I don't know. I do have a meeting with Dwight later this morning. Maybe he can figure out what to do about June. Personally, I think she'll come back if Dwight asks her, so I guess that's what I'll do-"

The first bell rang and interrupted Ronny's round-about apology. Marla Wexler immediately stood up and dragged Cathy Doherty off towards the door.

"Oh, Cathy, I bet all we'd have to do to get June back is mention who showed up to the meeting this morning."

She glanced over her shoulder at Seth, still lounging with his feet propped on a desk.

"And I bet she'd even take a 'B' in math to go out with Seth Knight. Don't you think so?" continued Marla, as they slid out the door and into the crowd.

~ ~ ~

Monday mornings have a particular style in the hallways of high schools everywhere, not at all the bustle of Friday afternoons or even the rapid, cooperative flow that you might find during the week. Rather, clumps of huddled cliques catching up secretively on all the weekend gossip, sandwiched in between dreary shufflers not nearly awake or even completely dressed after late Sunday nights and wild weekends. Here and there are the studious minority slumped in their textbooks and marching mysteriously through the sluggish Monday morning crowd, never glancing up, and yet not even hesitating as they thread their way unnoticed through the tangled maze of humanity. Then the occasional celebrity, maybe one of the exceptionally bad or perhaps the beautiful and popular will march straight through the throng as the Red Sea parts before them and the eyes watch in horror or fascination or envy.

One such person, Nick Yorchenko, or 'Butch' as he was always called, rounded the far corner, shuffling and swaying down the hallway like a leaky rowboat. He was obviously still under the influence of a typical weekend. Butch was easily the worst of all the troublemakers at school. People quickly got out of his way wherever he went. As he approached the Chronicle staff room, the door swung open and Seth stepped out directly in his path. Seth was another such person who turned heads. He looked at Butch with obvious disgust and stood resolute, still holding the door open. Butch peered through the morning haze and cackled at Seth,

"Well, pretty boy, you gonna be a reporter now or some-thin'?"

Seth, ignoring Butch's comment, glanced through the open doorway.

"C'mon Jann, I'll walk you to your class."

Jann Paris, the newspaper's graphic artist, emerged from the sanctuary of the room, obviously terrified of Butch. He licked his lips and belched.

"I'll walk you to your class, honey," he said, obviously taunting Seth.

The dull buzz of voices in the hallway was silenced, and every head was turned, waiting.

"Get lost scumbag," Seth said as he pushed his way past Butch and ushered his pretty friend along. He obviously wasn't afraid of Butch even though he was physically outmatched. To most people Butch looked gigantic, and they left him alone.

"What a jerk."

"Thank you, Seth," was Jann Paris' quiet reply as she clutched his arm with white knuckles.

~~~

The second bell rang. The signal meant that students had one minute to hustle off to homeroom before being marked tardy. The clumps of gossipers quickly broke up and the students raced off to class. Like sponges, the doorways soaked up the flow until, as the third bell rang to start the school day, only a few stragglers were left. Among them was Butch, hunched outside the restroom gobbling a candy bar.

CHAPTER FOUR

"Because of all the trouble we've been having with trash can fires lately, we've decided to have an assembly today on fire prevention. We've asked Mr. Gus Ford, a Portland City fireman, to give us a short presentation," said Dwight Stone, as he gestured to a tall, well-built man standing in the wings.

"I think we are all well aware of how vitally important this information is, especially in light of the recent rash of arson-related fires downtown the past few months, coupled with the childish insistence students on burning trash cans here at school. With these things in mind, let's all try our best to learn something here today. Shall we give Mr. Ford a warm Taft welcome?"

The crowd erupted in applause, mixed with the usual whistles and hoots.

"Thank you very much, young people."

Gus had a deep, rumbling, almost startling voice that silenced the crowd instantly. He had thick, red hair and a massive copper mustache that drooped down the sides of his mouth but when he smiled, his white teeth flashed. Despite his large bulky size, he looked friendly. His presentation consisted entirely of information on how to prevent accidental fires from getting started at home and at school, and in the use of fire extinguishers on the three types of fires. It was a concise talk that lasted only 15 minutes. When he was done, the student body again erupted in loud applause and Dwight dismissed them back to their third period classes.

Seth walked up to Dwight at the front of the auditorium as he sat on the edge of the stage, legs dangling, watching the people walking out.

"So, hot shot, you learn anything new?"

"Naw. Why, we gonna be tested?"

"Tell you the truth, Seth, I learned a lot. Who were you sitting next to?"

"Aw it wasn't that, Dwight, I just didn't get into the guy too much. Not only was he really dry, he had shifty eyes. He didn't even mention the arsonist downtown you know. Some exciting inside information would have at least made the speech a little tolerable. One of the first things you learn in speech class is to not be boring."

"Well, I guess I'd rather be just about anything in the world besides a fireman, Seth. Those guys are a special breed, facing danger the way they do every day."

"Yeah, I guess you're right."

"So, Seth, tell me how the newspaper thing is coming along. I haven't talked to you for a while now," Dwight said, adroitly changing the subject.

"Well... I think I'll need some more time to get used to the idea, Dwight. I sort of feel out of place there and I'm really not that close to any of those people, so..."

"Tell me this, my friend," Dwight said, looking at Seth with a solemn expression, "Who *are* you close to?"

The question took Seth off guard and he stood looking at Dwight with no answer at all. Seth's attention was suddenly diverted by Sylvia Skondberg, who floated by and touched him on the shoulder.

"Don't be late to class now, Seth," she said in her soft, low voice.

Seth gawked as she walked away. Dwight laughed at him and hopped off the stage, thumping Seth on the back.

"You'll find someone, Seth. Don't worry. Now let's get going."

~~~

As Monday marched slowly past, the insistent clumps of

gossipers gave way to a still sleepy yet more orderly flow, and by the time lunch was over the catching-up process was usually complete and the week was fully underway.

Jann Paris ate lunch with her usual fifth period art class friends, a group which normally included Seth. Today, however, he was off making the rounds.

"So, Jann, tell me all about Seth and Butch this morning, and how come he was at the chronicle with you and what's going on between you two anyway?"

A cross look flashed on Jann's usually serene face and she flicked her hair back in agitation.

"Aw, Mary, you know we're just friends. I've known Seth since we were kids."

"Well, I know."

"Funny thing. For some reason or other Seth joined the Chronicle staff this morning, although he sure didn't seem very excited about it. I can't figure out why he would even want to. It isn't very much fun this year."

"Well, what about Seth and Butch? Everybody's talking about that."

"Oh, Mary, that guy is so disgusting, and yet Seth didn't even flinch at him. He just ignored him and walked away. I really don't think Seth was afraid of Butch at all. He just started talking about the test on Friday in art class. I mean, I kept looking behind to see if Butch was following us or something. I sure felt a lot safer hanging on to Seth's arm-"

"You were hanging on to his arm?!"

"Oh, shut up Mary. I was just so scared of Butch-"

"I know. I know. Gosh, I wish they could do something about him. He's so dirty, and then the way he..."

The subject was cut short by the appearance of several members of the football team who were sauntering by, accompanied by a number of beautiful girls. The two girls silently watched them walk past. The popular boys wanted to be seen with the gorgeous girls. It was an almost indisputable fact of life. The only contradiction to that rule seemed to be Seth Knight. His olive skin and black hair was contrasted by bright blue eyes; eyes that almost didn't belong in a frame like his rugged face. They were soft, transparent, tender, yet always elusive, perhaps to protect the secret treasure of his heart. Despite this attractive exterior however, Seth had the reputation of talking to almost anyone at all. It didn't seem to bother him to be seen with the plain or even the outcast people.

Just then Seth strolled past the girls, talking to Holly Wilson, who was a genius in math but had a deformed back and very few friends. Seth had been known to actually visit Holly's house from time to time, perhaps after one of many surgeries to bring flowers, or for math tutoring, or just to say hello.

~ ~ ~

As the bell rang at the end of lunch, Travis West jogged over to his locker and, on impulse, grabbed his camera. He took the time to load a roll of film and have a few words with friends in passing, and then had to sprint across campus so he wouldn't be late for PE. As he rounded the corner of the industrial arts building to slip in the back door of the gym he saw a couple of people crouched in front of a trash can, so he instinctively snapped a quick succession of pictures before they saw him. Holding the book of matches was none other than Butch Yorchenko. A low whistle escaped Butch's lips and half a dozen of his gang appeared from behind the hedge and joined Butch and Rolly Howard, a small skinny boy with acne who was notorious as Butch's right hand man.

Butch advanced towards Travis with a scowl, backed by his gang.

"C'mon, big boy, just hand over the film like a nice jock."

Just then Seth trotted around the corner, obviously late, and stopped short.

"Keep outta this, pretty boy. Jus' go on to yer class now."

Seth saw the smoke rising up behind Butch and his gang and guessed the rest. There was a tense moment, each side sizing up

25

the other. The odds were obviously against Travis and Seth, but Butch certainly liked it better when it was only Travis. Nobody noticed that Greg had rounded the corner behind Travis and Seth.

"C'mon, jock, before you get hurt real bad. Jus' gimme the film an' get th' hell outta here."

"Come and get it, scum," Seth immediately replied. He glanced at Travis and was surprised. Travis was smiling as he said,

"Yeah, Nicky, you want it, you gotta take it."

Nobody ever called Butch by his real name.

"C'mon, guys, I want blood!" Butch growled between clenched teeth.

What happened next surprised everyone. Greg darted in from behind Seth and Travis like a tiger, grabbed Butch by his jean jacket and lifted his 200 pound bulk off the ground as easy as if lifting a bag of dirty laundry. He stood there breathing hard and staring at Butch, unsure of what to do. Nobody moved. The bell rang. Still nobody moved, and Greg continued to hold Butch off the ground with no apparent effort at all. Finally Greg tossed him like a stuffed toy towards his gang behind him and stamped his huge boot on the dead grass.

"GO AWAY!" he shouted, pointing and trembling with rage.

The gang all turned and walked away, only Butch bothering to glance back with a look of hate and desire for revenge smeared on his face.

"You'll get yours real soon... freak..." he muttered, rounding the corner.

CHAPTER FIVE

"Seth!" The loud yell echoed through the hall early Tuesday morning as Seth shuffled along, headed no place in particular.

"Seth, c'mere." Seth turned to see Travis trotting towards him, face flushed with excitement.

"Did you hear about the big fire last night?" Travis asked, out of breath.

"What fire? Where?"

Travis was beside himself.

"Downtown. I was listening to my dad's scanner and I heard this report of a fire, so he and I drove down there and I got the greatest pictures! You wouldn't believe it! I got there before the cops and some of the firemen too. After the cops got there the crowd got so big they wouldn't even let the press in. I got better pictures than any of 'em. Wait till ol' Ron sees this stuff."

Seth was impressed.

"Your old man's got a scanner, huh?"

"Yeah. I was just lucky Dad wasn't busy. He rarely lets me use his car so I'm sure I couldn't use it for something like that."

"We could just take my car man." Seth muttered.

"Let's go see if Mr. Wilson can develop this stuff, Seth."

As they walked towards the industrial arts building, Travis was chatting away about the fire and Seth mused on how different Travis was off the field.

"Probably had nothing to talk about before," he muttered to himself, thinking about how adamantly Dwight had defended Travis.

"Say what, Seth?"

"Huh? Oh nothing. I was just thinking out loud. You know man, I hardly know you at all. Why is that? We've played ball together for a long time now, you know," Seth said, blue eyes boring into Travis with fierce intensity.

"Yeah, I guess not too many people do know me very well. It's my own fault, mostly. I never know what to talk about, so I don't say anything. Actually, Seth, I've always admired the way you can carry on a discussion with anybody at all. How do you do that?"

Seth laughed loud, and it echoed through the tangle of buildings as they walked along. Travis listened to the echo and a warm smile crossed his face. Seth shook his head.

"I don't know, man. To me it's all fluff. Most of it, anyway. I must get it from my dad. He's awesome at it, only he actually says things that are worthwhile."

Seth paused and stared at Travis for a moment.

"You're pretty close to Dwight, aren't you?"

"Yeah, I guess I am. Why?"

"Nothing really. You're okay though, man." He slapped Travis on the back with another laugh. "Yeah. You're an okay guy."

When they got to the photography classroom, Mr. Wilson was just setting up the darkroom for the day and agreed to develop the roll of film.

"Too bad it's only black and white, Seth. The fire was awesome. It was this huge warehouse and it was totally covered with flames. I swear you could feel the heat from across the street. I overheard the firemen say something about arson too. Probably the same guy who lit all those other fires downtown."

They chatted a bit until Mr. Wilson came out of his darkroom holding the dripping negatives.

"These look just fine, boys, but I really won't have time to proof them 'til seventh period, okay?"

They scanned the negative strip and turned away disappointed.

"Okay, Mr. Wilson. Thanks a lot for your help."

The subject of pictures and newspaper articles quickly left

Seth's mind as they emerged from the industrial arts building and he caught sight of Sylvia Skondberg jogging around the track.

"Hey, Travis, I'll pick up those pictures with you after school, huh?"

"Sure, Seth."

Seth vaulted the low fence around the field and strolled over to the bleachers to watch Miss Skondberg running. Sylvia was the type of woman you didn't bother calling beautiful. Beautiful was almost an insult. A better word would be magnificent. She didn't seem to know it either. Most of the time she seemed almost unaware of her impact on men, even though heads would turn everywhere she went. This might have been due to her general preoccupation with life, or maybe her boyfriend of several years, or just her particular style.

To Seth however, she had one serious flaw. She belonged to someone else. She also seemed unaffected by Seth's lavish admiration of her. Unbeknownst to anyone, Seth had a journal full of poetry, much of it devoted to Sylvia. Perhaps someday she would be the first one to read it and see Seth Knight as no one ever had before. He just had to be sure she wouldn't ostracize him for it. Seth watched as Sylvia pushed extra hard on her last lap and, after walking around one more time to cool down, disappeared into the girl's locker room. The first bell invaded his daydream, and he trudged slowly off towards the main building.

~~~

After school and a short football practice, Seth and Travis headed over to Mr. Wilson's classroom to pick up the prints. He was stooped over the counter in his classroom studying them when the boys walked in. He was a tall, broad shouldered man with a thick mustache and a forehead deeply creased with his incessant scowl.

"Son, did you take these pictures at a fire somewhere?"

"Yeah! It was last night at this warehouse downtown. Hey, look at this one! With the crowd in the foreground it really gives you a perspective on how big the fire actually was. I swear Mr. Wilson, I'd never seen anything like it. It was horrible."

Mr. Wilson examined the photograph under his lens.

"Hard to tell on the contact sheet son, why don't you leave these here with me and I'll make a batch of three-by-fives. I do believe this shot with the crowd is clear enough to see the expressions on their faces. That should make an interesting study. You must have some fine equipment."

"Yes sir! Cost me a lot too. I worked all last summer to pay for it, but it sure was worth it." Travis beamed.

"Now what are these three shots here? Looks like hobos digging in a trash can or something."

This observation brought a chuckle to both Travis and Seth, because it was so close to the truth. Travis told Mr. Wilson about the episode with Butch's gang and how Greg had surprised them all. Mr. Wilson examined the three shots with renewed interest.

"Too bad you can't see the faces too well, although in this one, with the smoke coming up, it's plain as day what they're doin'. And Francovich going after that Butch character too? Imagine that. Well, fellas, you can pick these up first thing tomorrow morning."

"Sure thing! Thanks a lot Mr. Wilson."

Mr. Wilson stooped and peered at the pictures for some time after the boys had gone, muttering to himself.

~ ~ ~

Seth often walked to school instead of driving, as he lived close to the campus. It was a pleasant walk which, with only a minor detour, led him past the south side of the lake the town was named after. Today Seth took this detour because he had so much to think about, and he walked right past Greg's house, which happened to be just around the corner from his own home. As he passed by, the front door burst open and Greg clumped out.

"Hi, Greg!"

Greg looked up open mouthed.

"Uh, hullo, Seth."

Just then a brash voice rang out from inside Greg's house. "Gregory!"

Greg looked nervously over his shoulder, spat out a quick, "Bye, Seth!" and then stomped back into the house.

"Such a strange guy. Wonder what he's all about..." Seth thought as he strolled home.

~~~

Greg Francovich was indeed a strange character. Most people's minds are crowded with words and pictures racing by every waking moment. Things like rehearsed speeches, 'just in case I bump into so and so at lunch', or 'how am I going to explain this to Dad' with various abstract attempts, or even fantasy scenarios prompted by the rush of excitement over guess-who's body or some delicious meal or various combinations.

By comparison, Greg's mind was usually filled with numbers. In fact, Greg was pretty near genius in his ability to handle numbers. One could call it a photographic memory, but it was very specific. His one hobby, building models of old sail boats, was abstracted in his mind by an unconscious and almost involuntary numerical memory system which listed parts, colors, glue joints, trivia on the history of the ship and its crew, and any interesting, related information. This was how Greg remembered almost everything. He actually had an encyclopedia of information including dates, phone numbers, addresses, license plates, the total count of words in books, measurements of various areas, buildings and rooms and even people's ages, but he didn't know what to do with it all, so it kept stacking up. That evening, Greg lulled himself to sleep by recounting how many pairs of black shoes he had seen that day.

~~~

Late that evening a small, beat up car rolled up in front of Greg's house and parked. A thin, dark figure emerged from the parked car, the late night silence broken by the soft crunch of shoes in the frosty grass. He opened the trunk of his car, paused to light a cigarette, and withdrew six bottles, putting them on the ground beside the car. Then he placed the bottles in various spots around the house and got a roll of wire out of the car and ran wire from bottle to bottle until the wire went all the way around the house. After this, he unscrewed each of the lids and replaced them with corks connected to a device on the top and hooked the wire to the devices. Then he attached the end of the wire to a small box and, after making a quick adjustment, ran to his car and raced off into the night.

~~~

Usually Greg slept like a winter bear, but for some reason he woke up several times during the night. It was dark, chilly, and silent as a morgue. When he awoke this time, he'd been tossing and turning and his arm was as cold as a piece of meat underneath him. He flipped over with a grunt and massaged it to get the feeling back again.

Suddenly, just outside his window, he heard a soft clinking noise, then the crunching of footsteps in the frost on the front lawn. He froze in fear. He sat up in his bed and gripped at the blankets, torn between the desire to hide and the curious urge to look out the window. His breath sucked in with a gasp as the person's shadow from the dim street light flicked quickly past his drawn shades, huge and distorted. He decided to get up and peek out. As he threw the blankets back and stepped to the floor he heard the footsteps trot off, a car door slam and the car drive away. Just as he breathed a sigh of relief there was a loud boom and a bright flash by the garage door just outside his window, and the whoosh and glare of flames. He screamed. The black night was suddenly bright with fire, raging fierce around the garage. Greg's mind raced and whirled. He grabbed and clawed at his blankets, and his eyes were glued to the dancing, phantom flames reflected on his blinds. Finally, after what seemed like hours but was only half a minute, his father stumbled into his room from across the hall, still half asleep. In one instant, he saw the reflected flames outside, snapped to complete awareness and bounded over to Greg's bedside.

"Out, Greg. Now! We gotta get outta here!"

It was no use. He flung one of Greg's arms over his shoulders and dragged him out of bed and out of his room. He then called to Greg's mother,

"Betty! Up and outta here quick! The house is on fire!"

As soon as he had his family safely on the back lawn, he raced in the back door to the phone in the kitchen. His voice was calm and commanding as he relayed his address and name to the fire department. Then he rejoined his wife and Greg.

"Let's go around front and wait for the firemen."

As soon as they rounded the far side of the house they heard the howl of sirens in the distance. The garage was engulfed in flames and the rest of the house was quickly being threatened. Greg stood dumb and uncomprehending, weeping like an infant. The fire engine screamed around the corner and skid to a halt in front of the house. The firemen moved like precision machines, weaving in and out with hoses, barking orders back and forth, hauling equipment, and Greg's numerical mind grabbed onto this precise activity like a security blanket. Counting steps and firemen, sorting commands from responses, these were things he could hang on to. The tears stopped.

The firemen had the blaze controlled in just a few minutes and altogether out in ten, but it was fully half an hour before Tom Mancuso, the Lake Oswego chief, approached the family. For the longest time Chief Mancuso and police Lieutenant Biggs had been talking with the other firemen and walking around and around the house in deep discussion. Then they had split up, Lieutenant Biggs going over to his squad car and Chief Mancuso coming over to talk to the Francovich family, his soot-smeared face drawn with sorrow and anxiety.

"Frank... I'm so sorry... I don't know what to say."

"Tom, whaddya think started it? I'm always so careful with

rags and flammables out here; I gotta be 'cause I'm always out here workin'. Can you tell me what started it yet? Do you know?"

Mr. Francovich held himself tall, but his face showed every sign of despair, as if he expected his own negligence to be the cause of the blaze.

"That's just it, Frank. We're sure it wasn't your carelessness that started this thing, but it all looks so strange to us. We gone over and over what we found but it just doesn't make any sense at all..." He paused and fidgeted with his coat nervously.

"Tom, whaddya tryin' to tell me? Friend to friend here, Tom, we've known each other too long to mince words."

"That's just it, Frank. We found certain signs, but it just don't make any sense. Not with you folks, so I just can't make heads or tails of it, Frank. I just don't know what to say to you 'til I look further into it."

"Can't you tell me anything?"

"Frank, I'm not puttin' you off. No way. You just got enough on your mind without me adding to your worries with something that might be an old fool's notions. What I wanna to do is call the investigator they got on the downtown fires to come have a look first thing in the morning, if that's okay with you. You're a good friend, and I'd like to pull my weight and get an expert's opinion right away. How 'bout it, Frank? It's the least I can do for you."

"I trust you, Tom, so if that's what's best... now how... how's the house?"

"Well, the garage is a loss, Frank. It's gone. And Greg's room got scorched a little on the garage wall side, but we stopped it there. My men are the best, Frank, and If you lived in the city, it'd be a lot worse. You got a lot of smoke in there but we're pullin' it out with the fans. I think you'll have to put up in a hotel for a few days, maybe more. We'll know more in the morning. I could call the hotel on Main-"

A voice from behind them interrupted Tom's words. It was Seth's.

"They can stay with us. I'm Seth Knight, a friend of Greg's

from school. We live just around the corner and it's no problem at all. We have a spare room upstairs-"

"Thanks a lot son," Mr. Francovich cut in, "but I can't expect your folks to put my family up when-"

A deep, controlled voice interrupted from behind Seth.

"It would be far less than neighborly for us not to open our home to you sir. Gene Knight, Seth's father. Anything we can do to help would be genuinely fulfilling to my family, and offering you shelter is the least we could do. Please, you are very welcome. Would you do us the service of accepting?"

The tears trickled down Frank's cheeks. He held out his hand.

"Frank is my name sir, an' my family, well, we thank you. I don't know what to say."

Gene took charge.

"Seth, take Greg home while we finish up here, and help your mom set up the spare room. We'll be home in a few minutes."

Seth put his hand on Greg's shoulder, steered him away, and they walked away down the street in silence.

CHAPTER SIX

"Mornin', Dad. You sleep much?"

"Not too well. Your mother and I talked for a while after we went to bed. An event like last night makes you realize just how helpless you really are most of the time. How about you?"

"Me neither. What's for breakfast-" Seth was cut short by a commanding knock at the door.

"Awful early for someone to be coming by," Gene muttered.

A huge man, obviously an albino with his white hair, parchment skin and pink eyes that quivered, dressed in a black trench coat and reeking of nicotine stood at the door with a business card in his extended hand. It read, 'STERLING VINTON STRANGERSON: PRIVATE INVESTIGATOR' and gave a New York address.

"How can we help you Mr. Strangerson?" Gene said hesitantly.

The reply was in a deep, discordant voice.

"Francovich family staying here?"

"Yes, they are. How can we help you?" Gene said, with a note of impatience in his smooth speech.

"I'm investigating last night's fire. I have a few questions for 'em if it's possible."

"Please come in, sir. Care for a cup of coffee?"

"Yeah, sure. Mind if I smoke?"

"I'd prefer if you didn't, Mr. Strangerson."

"Call me Hike. And your name?"

"Gene. Gene Knight. This is my son, Seth."

They shook hands and walked into the kitchen.

"Have a seat, ah, Hike, and I'll see if I can rouse the family."

Seth eyed this man suspiciously as he poured him a cup of coffee. A long, nasty scar on his cheek accentuated the hypnotic, quivering eyes that now appeared to be lavender in the blue kitchen.

Seth set the cup of coffee in front of him silently.

"Thanks, kid."

Seth frowned at the 'kid'. Hike picked up the cup and drank it down in a single gulp as Mr. Francovich shuffled around the corner holding Hike's business card.

"You got questions for me sir?"

"You Anthony Francovich?"

"Call me Frank."

"Call me Hike. I don't got great news for you, Frank. I been out to your place this morning, and I talked to the fire chief last night. All told, you been hit by an arsonist. I believe it could be the same one that's been doin' the downtown fires because the modus operandi is the same. I don't know how much you found out last night, but you people are lucky to be alive. This guy uses what we call simultaneously triggered detonators. I been on this guy's trail for years, and that's what he always uses. He screwed up last night though. I never seen him screw up before either. He had your place surrounded but only the garage side went off. Loose wires. Otherwise your place'd be nothin' but cinders."

"Why would a criminal burn down my house sir? It's absurd."

"I don't know, Frank. That's what I'm here to find out. I never seen him hit anything smaller than a warehouse before..."

Seth interrupted the discussion.

"I hate to disagree with you, Mr. Strangerson, but I happen to believe you're wrong and I'm positive I know who did this."

Seth stood with crossed arms, looking calmly at this huge man who'd had the audacity to call him 'kid'. The shadow of a sneer darted across Hike's face as he turned to face Seth, eyes flitting like gnats.

"The reason I'm on this case is I'm the best. You got that?

The best in the country at what I do an' I don't take kindly to school boys tellin' me how to do my job. Understand?"

He turned back to Frank, expecting his speech to have its usual effect of intimidation, but Seth stood resolute, feeling goaded rather than intimidated. He chose his words carefully, to attack as well as inform.

"Listen, pal, we got a torch at our school too. A serious dirtbag. Greg made a fool out of him a couple of days ago by tossing him right on his butt in front of his whole gang. So if I were you, I'd look this guy up first thing. If I know Butch Yorchenko, that fire was lit by him."

Seth leaned back against the wall and sipped his coffee complacently, feeling rather smug about his speech. It had indeed been effective, too. Hike Strangerson wasn't accustomed to his authority being questioned in the least as he was usually surrounded by local fireman and policeman types who had none of his expertise. Here was a bright young man who had no job at stake and didn't have to respect him. It made Hike defensive.

"Listen son, I've spent the last seven years on this guy's trail. Almost 100 fires in five cities, so I believe I know what I'm talking about, but if you have some information I don't have, I certainly would appreciate it."

Maybe it was being called 'kid', or maybe it was Hike's haughty, condescending attitude or perhaps it was Greg shuffling around the corner just now in his pajamas looking like he'd spent the night on a park bench, but whatever it was, something in Seth switched on in response to the crazy chain of events he'd gone through the last few days and he found he was being seriously challenged to step up to the plate. *'Maybe you're not so hot, Mr. Detective. Maybe I can show you a thing or two about catching criminals',* he thought to himself. Greg had become the underdog, and Seth had always been drawn to help underdogs all his life. He also had a wild notion that there was much more to Greg than one first observed; something that needed discovering.

As Gene walked into the room after Greg, he immediately sensed the tense atmosphere and responded.

"Greg, this is Hike Strangerson, the investigator for the fire department. He's got a couple of questions for you about last night. Why don't you sit down here and make yourself at home? Can I get you some coffee or milk or something?"

"Milk," he answered quietly. Gene turned to get the milk and Hike turned to Greg with his strange, quivering stare.

"I heard you had a run-in with one of the school hoodlums. Why don't you tell me about it?"

Greg blushed and looked to his dad for help.

"Go on son, it's okay."

There was a long pause as he drank his milk in loud gulps. Then he sat and collected his thoughts.

"Well... I come around the corner at school and I see Seth an' Travis standing there and Butch was saying bad things to 'em. Then Butch says that he wants the film and you see sir, Seth and Travis are my friends. I don't like Butch anyhow because he always makes fun of me, so when I seen him go after my friends I got real mad... and so I... I told him to go away, and then he left."

Seth chuckled softly at the obvious omission of the best details of the scene.

"Let me tell you what really happened. We've been having lots of trash can fires lately, and it just so happened that my football partner, Travis West got a couple of candid photographs of Butch and some other losers right in the act of lighting a can on fire. These guys decided that Travis should give up his camera. I showed up just after it happened and evened the odds up a little bit, but when these punks made a move for us, Greg darted in from behind Travis and me and picked Butch right off the ground and held him there like a toy. This guy is an easy 200 pounds too. Finally Greg tossed Butch back at his crew and yelled at 'em to go away. It was radical. These guys were so shocked they just walked off in a daze. I was real proud of Greg, but this Butch is a nasty dude. Downright brutal when he's mad I've heard, so there's no doubt in my mind that the fire was lit by Butch."

Greg was obviously embarrassed and almost ashamed until his father put his hand on his shoulder and squeezed hard.

"You done real good, son. I'm proud o'you."

Hike cut in.

"If I could get a phone and address of this character I'll look into it myself right away."

Greg's face fell blank for a moment, mentally computing, and he recited the address and phone number rapidly like a rehearsed speech. Hike quickly jotted it down, not really noticing, but Seth and his father reacted with surprise. Just then, a knock at the door broke their train of thought.

"Well, I'd best be goin', folks. Thanks for your help here, an' I'll be gettin' in touch with this Butch fella."

They all walked out to the front door and found Gunther outside. Hike slid out of the door while Gunther gawked at him, open mouthed.

"C'mon in, Gunther. You had breakfast?" Seth said, holding open the door for him. His eyes were as wide as saucers as he walked in the door.

"Seth called me this morning, Greg, so I came right over. I went by your place too. It's trashed. Who was that guy. Is he an albino? What's he doing here? So what's for breakfast?"

He was chattering like a nervous monkey. Seth cut in on him.

"Gunther, I don't believe you've met my father, Gene. This is Gunther, Taft's resident Einstein. He and Greg are best friends so I thought I'd give him a call this morning. You had breakfast, Gunther?"

"No, I haven't. Nice to meet you, sir. I understand you're a psychologist."

"Yes, Gunther, that's correct. What is your field of study may I ask?" Gene said with a twinkle in his eye.

"Oh, I guess right now I'm concentrating on mathematics, computer programming and chemistry, but I'm not settled as of yet on a specific field of pursuit. Still getting the basics out of the way, sir."

"Would you care for some breakfast, Gunther?" Gene asked politely with a wink at Seth.

"Sure. Thanks. I'm starved. But who was that guy just now?

He looked like a big ghost. Gave me the creeps."

They all walked into the kitchen as Seth explained.

"Some hotdog private eye from New York who thinks Greg's house was hit by the same torch that's responsible for the downtown fires. I guess he's been chasing this guy all over the country. I think he's got a real ego problem. I told him about the Butch scene at school Monday and so he's off looking for Butch. I bet 20 bucks it was Butch and not that other guy. I hope Butch fries for it too. He's disgusting."

Just then Kelly Knight, Seth's mother walked in. Kelly had jet black hair that hung in long silken waves to the middle of her back and deep green eyes that never seemed to either blink or look away from you.

"I suppose you men expect me to cook your breakfast... my, our ranks have grown even more. I don't believe I've ever met you, young man. I'm Kelly Knight."

"Gunther Stern, ma'am." Gunther reached out and gently took Kelly's hand. Seth chimed in.

"To tell you the truth, Mom, Dad was planning on cooking for everyone, weren't you Dad?"

Gene looked at him with mischievous smile and reached into his pocket and withdrew a coin, flipping it into the air.

"Call it!"

"Heads!"

"Sorry, Seth. Tails. You cook. Ha!"

"You clean then, Pop. I've got school today!."

Seth turned into the kitchen to start breakfast and Greg's mother joined the group as they wandered over to the dining room table.

"I hope everybody likes scrambled eggs and potatoes, 'cause that's what I'm cookin' today. How many eggs can you eat, Greg?"

Greg's father laughed and Greg blushed.

"Greg can eat as many as you can cook, Seth. An' then some. This kid costs a fortune to feed!" Everybody chuckled, and the smell of cooking breakfast filled the house as Seth got the meal going.

~ ~ ~

Later, as Seth sat quietly eating his breakfast, he listened to the chatter of discussion and hypotheses going around the table regarding the fire, and he mused on how his life had taken such a big turn since the little fire extinguisher episode in the cafeteria the week before. With his three new friends, he had a rapidly growing interest in reporting, and now he was getting involved with a serious crime investigation and perhaps a major criminal as well. Seth looked at Gunther and Greg across the table. What a bond the two of them had, and between two people who were so drastically different. Then Seth remembered Greg's performance with Butch's telephone number.

"Gunther."

The conversation died and all eyes turned to Seth. He had the uncanny ability to get people's attention.

"You and Greg are best friends aren't you?"

"Sure! How come?"

"What do you know about Greg knowing everybody's phone number?"

Gene zeroed in like a hawk. He'd temporarily forgotten the incident earlier and had a keen professional interest in it. Gunther scratched his head thoughtfully.

"Greg can remember huge amounts of information as long as it has something to do with numbers. You should see how much he knows about his model boats. It's awesome! And I bet he could tell you anyone's phone number and address in the school, too, and what page in the phone book it's on. Oh yeah, and then there's dates. He can tell you what day any date in history falls on. It's really incredible."

"I just wish he could get it to work at school. We had the dickens of a time gettin' him out of all them special classes, but he's just not cuttin' it in the real world yet," muttered Greg's father through a mouthful of toast.

"I'm sure, Frank, assuming this ability of Greg's is as extensive as it appears, we could develop a system for Greg that would help with a wide variety of information. I'd really appreciate doing some testing as long as it would be all right with you Greg."

Gene turned his comforting, professional 'trust me' look on Greg, who was three shades of red.

"What do you think?"

"Well, that would be fine sir, long as it's not no trouble."

"Not at all Greg. I did a lot of reading on this kind of memory in school. It's a rare phenomenon, and you'd be doing me a big favor by giving me the opportunity to study first-hand what I've only been able to read about in books before."

"Well, okay sir, long as it don't hurt much."

"More like playing games and talking," Gene laughed.

Seth always enjoyed watching his father talk to people, or 'work' as he called it. He had a wonderful ability to make friends with anyone, and quickly. It was a process Seth never got tired of watching.

Just then Stacy, Seth's sister, walked into the dining room rubbing her eyes.

"Is there anything left for me?"

Gunther sat with open mouth and gawked, first at Kelly, then at Stacy, who was like a carbon copy of her mother, with shorter hair.

Seth laughed.

"You're on your own sis. By the way, have you ever met Gunther here? He's a good friend of Greg's."

She glanced at Gunther quickly.

"Nice to meet you. I'm starved. Didn't you cook me anything, Mom?"

Kelly smiled and said,

"Seth did the cooking for us this morning, so-"

"Yuck. Never mind. I'll make my own." She whirled out of the dining room.

Seth glanced down at his watch and spoke up.

"Hey! It's getting late. We gotta get going. Now, if you guys hurry up, I'll drive you to school. And by the way, why don't we keep this business of Butch and the private eye to ourselves? What do you think, Dad?"

"I think that's not only wise, but really very necessary. I'm a bit surprised that Hike didn't mention it himself. It's also probably prudent for the time being that we keep the location of the Francovich family to ourselves too, okay?"

Everyone agreed and then bustled off to get their day under way.

CHAPTER SEVEN

As soon as Seth arrived at school that morning he spotted Travis in the crowded hallway, standing at his locker with an armful of textbooks.

"Hurry man, into homeroom. This is important stuff."

He ducked into their mutual class and selected two chairs in the far corner of the room. Travis shuffled in afterwards and plopped himself down.

"So what's the big deal?" Travis asked casually.

"You hear about the fire last night?"

"Downtown?"

"No. Here in town. It was Greg Francovich's house."

"Really?"

"Yeah. I was there too. They live just around the corner from us. We got his family staying with us in the spare room while they fix the damage."

"How bad was it?"

"Mostly the garage, but that's not all. Six o'clock this morning this private detective comes bangin' on my front door claiming the fire was lit by the downtown torch. The house was surrounded with fire bombs, but only a few of 'em went off or the whole family could've been killed."

Travis' jaw dropped open.

"You're kidding!"

"No."

The two of them sat in silence for a few moments while Travis thought about this shocking information.

"What's even worse is, I think it was Butch that did it, man.

After what Greg did to him the other day, I wouldn't put it past the pig. I told the private eye about Butch and he's out looking into it right now."

"What's this private eye all about?"

"Tell you the truth Travis, I don't like the guy at all."

"What do you mean?"

"I'm not sure. Really strange guy. I guess he's been following the arson all over the country. I don't know, Travis. I just didn't like him one bit, and I think I'm going to look into this thing myself."

"Really?"

"Yeah, and I wanna keep it really quiet too, even from Dwight. I don't want anyone to know what I'm doing for now, 'cause it just might get around. You know what I mean?"

"I sure do, but I can't believe Butch would try and kill a whole family Seth. I just can't believe it."

They were interrupted by the second bell.

"I gotta find out. That's for sure. I better get to my locker before it's too late." Seth vaulted over his chair and scrambled out the door.

~ ~ ~

After homeroom, Travis trotted over to the industrial arts building to pick up his fire photographs from Mr. Wilson.

"Mr. Wilson? Hello?"

The room was empty and the door to the darkroom was ajar so he stepped inside and flipped on the lights. True to his word, Mr. Wilson had printed the whole roll. Glancing at his watch, Travis scooped up the prints and trotted off to class.

~ ~ ~

Mr. Wilson hit the ceiling when he came back to the classroom a short time later.

"Johnson! Where are the prints I left here? Johnson!"

Armin Johnson, Mr. Wilson's teacher's aide came scrambling through the back door and into the darkroom.

"Pardon me, sir?"

"Where are the prints I had laying right here?"

"I don't know, sir. I just stepped out to visit the restroom a minute ago and..."

"I just developed 'em 15 minutes ago and they're already missing. You didn't see anyone in here?"

"No sir."

"Fine. I'll find 'em myself, Johnson."

He paused and waited for Armin to leave the darkroom, then slid open a shallow drawer under the counter and withdrew a large photograph.

"At least they didn't get this one," he muttered as he studied the photograph. It was an enlargement of the photograph Travis had taken of the fire with the crowd in the foreground.

~~~

By lunchtime, almost everyone in the school had heard about the Francovich fire, and as is usually the case with stories spread via word of mouth, most accounts were grossly exaggerated. Dwight realized the importance of accurate information, not only to save Greg a lot of embarrassment, but also to keep the curious crowds away from their house, so he sent a memo to all the sixth period classes. It read;

'As you may have heard, the house of Greg Francovich, a senior here at Taft was damaged last night in a fire. Fortunately nobody was injured and due to the quick response of our own Lake Oswego Fire Department, the damage was largely confined to the garage. Please respect the privacy of the Francovich family in this time of stress and refrain from spectating. Thank you for your sensitivity. Dwight D. Stone'

The memo was surprisingly effective.

~~~

After lunch ended and he was on his way to PE, Travis stopped by the industrial arts building to Mr. Wilson's class. As he stepped into the classroom, Mr. Wilson emerged from the back supply room.

"Hi, Mr. Wilson!"

Travis glanced past Mr. Wilson into the open door of the supply room and, on the steel shelf against the wall was a dozen gallon jugs filled with liquid and sealed by odd looking cork stoppers.

Mr. Wilson glared at Travis and replied tersely,

"What can I do for you?" as he slammed the supply room door shut.

"Well I just wanted to thank you for printing that roll for me. I picked it up this morning..."

"That was you, eh?" he said, eyeing Travis suspiciously.

"Yes sir. I would have left a note but I was running late."

"Hmm! Seems to me you modern kids are always running late and sticking your noses where they don't belong, but who listens to an old man anymore? Those pictures satisfactory, young man?"

"Yes sir. Thanks very much."

Travis trotted off to PE, somewhat puzzled by Mr. Wilson's peppery behavior.

~ ~ ~

After football practice, Seth and Travis strolled out to Seth's car in the parking lot. In the far corner of the lot was a half-dozen of Butch's gang, lounging around Rolly Howard's beat up Pinto, smoking cigarettes, but without Butch present, the gang seemed rather harmless.

"This yours?" Travis asked with a grin, pointing to Seth's car.

Seth drove a red 1963 Dodge Dart two door with a black interior and a black vinyl top. He always kept it clean and waxed, and it ran like new. It had taken a year of weekends to restore his car and Seth was proud of it.

"Cool, huh? Hey, you got time to come over for a coke or something?"

"Well, I'd like to Seth, but I gotta catch a bus in a few minutes so I guess I'll take a rain check."

"How about I give you a ride home apeman?"

"Sure!"

"Then let's go!"

When they got home, they found Gunther sitting in the family room at the game table listening to Gene and Greg having a discussion. It was a cozy room with a thick carpet and a small fireplace and Gene invariably chose this room for any informal discussions or interviews. Gene and Greg were involved in the process of learning about Greg's memory.

Seth and Travis stomped into the house, laughing, and disrupted the interview.

"Howdy... oh sorry Pop, didn't know you were busy."

"That's okay, son, we're almost done for the day."

"Dad, I don't think you've met Travis West from the team. Travis, this is my dad, Gene Knight."

"Nice to meet you Travis. I've seen you play, and I must admit that I'd hate to run into you on the football field."

They all laughed.

"By the way, can we count on you for dinner tonight Travis? Gunther has already agreed to stay, so why not make it a party?"

"Sure, thanks!"

"Excellent. I suppose I'd better get cooking then. Tonight is my night."

Gene walked out whistling and Travis spoke right up.

"You know Seth, I've been thinking about it all day, and I decided that I should help you look into Greg's house."

There was a long, silent pause. Seth's intense eyes bored into Travis' face. Gunther and Greg both turned and stared at Travis and Seth with open mouths. They were as yet unaware of Seth's interest in investigating the crime. All four of the boys were somehow aware that they stood at an important threshold.

"Really? How come?"

"Well, for one thing, Greg did both of us a mighty big favor by stopping that fight with Butch and the way I figure it, you could probably use a little help. And besides, he's a fellow Taft Bulldog and a friend too. What do you think?"

There was a long pause as Seth rubbed his stubbly chin and paced the floor.

"Well, if it *was* Butch, and I'm pretty sure of that, our crackpot private eye won't want to get involved. He's hot on the trail of the downtown man and this is just local news to him. Even if he did decide to follow it up, I think we can do a better job. I think the guy is burned out or something. You'd know what I meant if you met him. I guess if you want to help it would great. I'd hate to run into Butch and his gang all by myself some night. Sure, we should work together on this thing."

Gunther chimed in.

"How about me and Greg? We could help too you know."

"Gunther, you're a little young to be chasing after Butch Yorchenko. He'd make hamburger out of you."

"Well, I could always do other things, Seth. I have a computer at home and there are lots of ways of getting really useful information with it. Sometimes I can get information that can't be gotten any other way. If you guys are going to be doing detective work, you have to have a computer, and that's all there is to it. This is 1990 and everything is stored on computers nowadays."

Gunther paused and stood up, facing Seth with his hands on his hips.

"Seth, I am really good at getting access to almost anything stored on almost any computer, anywhere. Besides, I really want to help Greg and his family any way I can and if you two are doing something it makes it a lot easier for me to help out than if I tried to do something on my own, you know?"

"Well, I guess that would be okay, Gunther, as long as you kept your nose out of trouble. What do you think about all this, Greg?"

Greg had been silent with his hands folded in his lap staring at the floor. He looked up with tears and a fierce, almost frightening rage burning in his eyes. All he could do was nod his head. The four boys looked at each other with a grim determination painted on their faces.

Seth's eyes dimmed as he momentarily ruminated on the somewhat prophetic challenge about leadership that had come from Dwight Stone just a few days earlier. His life was rapidly changing. He looked up at the other boys with a flashing smile of confidence.

"Good. We need to get a plan of attack going then, and I have a great place to start."

Gene knocked on the door and poked his head in.

"Phone call for Greg."

Greg walked out and came back in only a few moments later.

"Gee, Seth. That was Hike. He told me that Butch was arrested last night for drunk driving and was in jail when the fire was lit. I guess he didn't do it then. What are we going to do now?"

There was a long pause. All you could hear was the regular breathing of the four boys.

"I can't see as it makes any difference Seth, really. I'm still in if you are," Travis said reassuringly.

"Me too," Gunther added softly.

"Well guys," Seth said suddenly, raising his head and startling them all with his intense, blue eyes.

"It looks like we've got a real criminal to chase instead of just a punk. I'm all for it, too!"

The boys erupted into a chorus of cheers and they all gathered around Greg and thumped him on the back. Seth interrupted their celebration.

"Okay guys. We need a plan. I know I've never done anything like this before and I doubt that anyone else has either. Who's got any ideas?"

He got a tingle down his spine as he said this because of Dwight's recent challenge about leadership. He felt as though he was being drawn into a whole new life of excitement and adventure, and that some kind of portal into this new life had already been crossed. If only he could remember just when this adventure had really begun.

Gunther interrupted his thoughts.

"We need information. I would suggest collating any data we now have and pushing for more, as much as possible. You never know what will turn up."

Gunther's thin voice contrasted sharply with his authoritative words. Seth responded.

"Okay Gunther. Let me tell you what I know. We got a criminal who's lit almost 100 fires in 5 cities the last 7 years according to Hike. That would make this guy pretty new in town, but how new I don't know."

"I'll take notes," Travis volunteered.

"Cool, Travis. Then we've got the bombs this guy uses. According to Hike it's always the same thing; bottles of gasoline ignited off by an electronic detonator attached to the top of the bottle."

Travis' face wrinkled into a frown and he gripped his forehead in his thick fingers, thinking.

"You know Seth, I noticed something strange at school... I guess it sounds crazy but.... Oh never mind. It's too stupid."

"When you exclude all the variables that are impossible, whatever remains, however improbable, is the truth. Sherlock Holmes." Gunther was proud of his quote and Travis gave in.

"Okay fine. Seth, did you notice Mr. Wilson acting weird the other day over those pictures?"

"No, not really. He's neurotic anyhow, from what I hear. Why?"

"Well, I noticed it, especially today when I picked up the prints. Real jumpy or something. Plus, when I walked into his class just before PE to thank him I saw a bunch of gallon bottles in his supply room, filled with some kind of liquid and they all had weird looking stoppers in them. It's probably a long shot I know. Does anybody know how long he's been at school?"

Nobody knew.

"Well, we'll just have to find out, won't we?" Seth said.

"Other than that, I don't know a thing. What now Gunther?"

"Well, what comes to mind is to gather as much police file information as we can on this guy. After 7 years, there must be a ton of data out there. I'll just have to do a little hacking through their computers, that's all. We could probably round up stuff that ghost of a private eye doesn't even know. I'll get on that right away. Plus, Greg and I could get together with, uh, what's his name again?"

"Strangerson."

"Well, I'll just call him The Ghost. We'll meet with him and see what we can learn. I'm sure he wouldn't suspect a couple of innocent kids like me and Greg now, would he?" Gunther said with his little boy look on his face.

"That sounds great, Gunther. Meanwhile, Travis and I can keep an ear glued to his dad's scanner and run downtown whenever we hear about another fire. Travis can continue to take pictures, too. By the way, do you have those pictures from Wilson?"

Travis withdrew the black and white prints from his backpack and began passing them around. The boys were struck silent by the awesome destruction of the fire, literally consuming the old, massive warehouse. The size of the fire was dramatized in the one photograph with the crowd in the foreground, their faces painted with grim fear and the fire trucks parked like toys in front of the massive building behind them. This photograph was a stern reminder of the serious task they were undertaking.

"We might end up with quite a collection of these before we're through, Seth. What should we do with them? I can shoot pictures all day long," Travis observed.

"They should be organized. Let Greg do it. Number and memorize them. You never know." Gunther chimed in.

Greg's face lit up at the prospect of his being useful. Seth pounced on the idea.

"Great! How about it, Greg?"

"Sure! That's okay."

"Okay, guys, we're cookin'. I'm going to look into Wilson and we need to find out how long the torch has been in town."

"Seth, between Greg and I, we'll get what we can out of the Ghost for you. I'm going to start a database right away on my computer so we can keep all our information organized."

"Great. All we need now is patience and a little luck, guys. And all I need is a little supper. I'm dying!" With that, the boys tumbled out of the family room into the kitchen to see what Gene was cooking.

CHAPTER EIGHT

It was one o'clock on Friday morning. Two dark figures slid silently across the front parking lot of Taft High School. They paused on the steps of the large auditorium just to the left of the main entrance and melted into the shadows around the left side of the auditorium. All along the side of the auditorium, the oldest part of the school complex, ran a low hedge. The two figures crept silently along the asphalt walk towards the rear of the building. Just before they rounded the back of the building into the lunch court they paused at a small, inconspicuous window, well hidden by a large bush.

"Greg, you wait here behind this bush. I'll get what we need and bring it out here. Otherwise, don't move. Okay?"

"Sure, Seth." He wriggled his bulk into the bush to wait. Seth softly slid open the window and vaulted into the opening.

"Gimme the box now, Greg."

Greg reached up and handed him a small cardboard box from behind the bush. Seth was in a tiny backstage restroom in the auditorium that very few people knew about. He had left the window unlocked that day for this mission. He strolled across the stage, hopped down, and crossed through the side door into the hallway. So far so good. As he closed the door behind him he strained his ears for any sound of the night watchman who by this time could be asleep. You just couldn't be too careful.

Seth quickly set off down the hall for the front of the school. He had to move fast because the night lights were on and there was no place to hide. He rounded the corner to the front hall and trotted over to the office doors, checking them as he went. All the offices were locked so he crossed to the receptionist's office. That door had no lock. Seth went in, shut the door and walked quickly over to her desk. It was locked as well so he rolled the chair back and squatted down behind the desk. As he did so, he accidentally nudged the chair behind him and it rolled back on the old wooden floor and thumped into the wall. He froze. The night watchman had been rounding the corner out in the hallway at that very moment. Seth saw his flashlight switch on and shine in the window of the dark office. The doorknob rattled and the door slowly swung open as the beam of the flashlight sliced through the middle of the dark room. Seth's heart pounded as he carefully worked the lid of the cardboard box open with his gloved hand from behind the desk.

"Who's there?"

The voice of the watchman quavered in the darkness as he reached for the light switch. Seth had to time his diversion just right. As the watchman flicked on the light, Seth quickly withdrew his hand from the box clutching a large, white rat and set it on the floor. He flicked the rat on the back with his forefinger as he let it go and it squeaked and scampered across the floor, past the watchman.

"Holy mackerel!!" the man yelped, as he leaped for a nearby chair.

"Big enough to take on a dog," he muttered, as he climbed down from the chair and left the office, shutting the light off and closing the door behind him.

After a minute, Seth resumed his mission. He withdrew a small, leather pouch from his pocket and took out a pair of tiny tools to open the lock on the desk. It was open in only a matter of seconds and he reached in, withdrew a key on a large ring, then quietly stood up and crossed to the door, listening intently before he opened it up. He quickly crossed the hallway and inserted the key into the lock on the main office. The door swung open and Seth stepped inside. He crossed the room to a large filing cabinet, rummaged around in it for a minute, and withdrew a manila folder. Meanwhile, Greg was, of course, sound asleep in the bush.

Fortunately, he wasn't snoring yet.

Later, as Seth's head emerged from the window Greg started a soft rumbling snore that usually signaled a freight train to come. Seth reached down and tapped Greg lightly on the head from his perch.

"Greg!" he hissed. Greg's head snapped up from his chest and he was wide awake, something that usually didn't happen once he fell asleep at night.

"I got it Greg! You sure you can remember all this stuff, man?"

"Yeah. Sure, Seth. Just show it to me and it'll be okay."

Seth handed him the file and Greg got that funny, distant look in his eyes as he scanned the pages inside with a flashlight. After a very short time he handed the file back to Seth.

"What's wrong, Greg? You can't read it or something?"

"I'm done, Seth. You can put it back now."

"You're kidding me!"

"No. I'm done. It's okay Seth, you can put it back now. I won't forget nothing."

The scrape of a footstep interrupted Greg. Seth hissed for Greg to be quiet and ducked his head down. The night watchman came whistling around the corner, swinging his flashlight in circles on the asphalt. As luck would have it, his light happened to stray up to the opened window as he passed the bush.

"Would ya look at that! Some dope left the window opened."

He began pushing his way into the bush to close it, but paused just as he was about to step on Greg's foot.

"Well, might as well get it from the inside," he muttered. He backed out of the bush and resumed his patrol.

Greg was literally faint with fear, but Seth, using his head, had made a quick exit as soon as the watchman had walked away, to replace the pilfered file. He was back in less than two minutes, but to poor Greg, it seemed like an hour. As Seth squeezed out of the window, he whispered,

"Okay Greg, let's get out of here quick."

They trotted down the asphalt path to the street and ran across to Seth's car.

"Gee, Seth, I never been at school at night before. It's creepy," Greg said as they stood by the car, looking at the school across the street.

"I guess I'm used to it, Greg. I go there all the time at night to think. I especially like the stage at night. Lots of energy, but nobody there to bother you. I usually write a lot."

"What do you write, Seth?"

"Oh, nothing much."

They hopped into the car and headed home.

~ ~ ~

While Seth and Greg had been at the school on their mission, Gunther had been busy on his own kind of adventure. He sat in front of his computer, the glow of the screen shining eerily on his face as he worked to gain entrance to the City's computer files without being noticed. To Gunther, at 13 years old, it was just about the most exciting thing he could imagine. Beads of perspiration gathered on his forehead as he tried several different entrance codes, but nothing seemed to work. Suddenly, he recalled a brief conversation he had with a hardware engineer at an electronics show the summer before. A strange combination of keys, all pressed down at the same time would gain entrance to any system, as long as the city was using the brand of server this man had engineered, because he had built the quirk into it himself. Gunther strained his memory to remember the right combination of keys. After several failed attempts he remembered the code and tried it out and it worked like a charm. Now all he had to do was figure out the right file name for the arsonist and download whatever came up, as he had plenty of time to read it later. He started with 'ARSON', but it was too general, and gave him nothing. He tried 'STRANGERSON' and had similar luck. He then called up a general menu of file names and began scrolling through them. After several minutes of scanning the gibberish on the screen, Gunther had jotted down several files that looked promising. He opened the first one. It was a background file on Hike and on an impulse; he saved it to his disk. The next was a statistical overview on arson crimes in the last 20 years. The next couple of files were even more disappointing.

Gunther began to get nervous. If someone at the police station were to notice what he was doing, he might not be able to disengage in time and he would potentially get caught. This kind of hacking was certainly a lot more serious than peeking at the school records or the library's files for an obscure book title. He could get in real trouble for this. His imagination began to work overtime. He decided to only look at one more file, and then call it a night. After glancing at the last file he broke into a big smile. It was an overview on the arsonist's activities, listing all sorts of information. Gunther could hardly repress a giggle as he started loading the information to his disk. The disk hummed away as the information poured in.

Suddenly there was a glitch on the screen. He froze in fear. Had someone noticed his activity? He broke out in a cold sweat and his trembling finger was poised over the master power switch on his computer's surge protector that would shut everything down instantly. The glitch disappeared and he relaxed a little. The disk drive hummed away for a little while longer and then he was through. He safely disconnected from the City's computer and stood up to take a deep breath. The back of his shirt was soaked with sweat and his hands were still trembling as he reached down and turned his system off. There was plenty of time later to study the file he had just pilfered. Now was a great time for a bowl of ice cream.

~ ~ ~

The next morning Seth called Gunther on the phone bright and early to find out what kind of luck he'd had the night before and to share a brief description of his success with Greg. They decided to have another meeting.

"So, you and Greg get together after school and get all this stuff written down where we can look at it. We can get together Saturday morning at my place and go over what we've turned up. If I get a chance I'm going to do a little more snooping at school today and see if I can find out anything else about Wilson. Wouldn't it be ironic if he really was the torch?"

"I'll have a printout of everything we have to date at the meeting Seth, okay?"

"Yeah. That is going to help a great deal, Gunther. I better get going now. See you at school maybe, okay?"

"Yeah."

~ ~ ~

Other than being a typical gloomy October day, it was also Halloween, and it started off being anything but typical as people began showing up in their costumes. Most people had the good sense to wear something that wouldn't be a complete nuisance all day long, but one person, gender unknown, showed up in a huge Godzilla suit and another person on stilts was a ten foot tall Frankenstein. They both got sent home to change, along with several others who had less-than-good taste.

"Well, to tell you the truth, Travis, I'd forgotten all about Halloween until I saw Godzilla this morning," Seth mused in their homeroom class.

"Are you going to the party tonight after the game?"

"I wouldn't miss it for anything," Travis replied. "I love Halloween. You can be anyone you want to be. Do you remember the Martian last year that nobody could guess? That was me. And you know what? Nobody will figure me out this year either. Not even you, wise guy."

"So why don't you tell me, then?"

"My lips are sealed," Travis said with a big smile.

"Well anyway, you doing anything tomorrow morning?"

"Naw. What's up?"

Seth looked around the classroom casually and then winked at Travis.

"Oh, I don't know. Nothing really. Why don't you come over

for a while? Shoot some pool or something?"

"Sure. What time?"

"Any time. Breakfast is at 9:30 or so on weekends. I'm cookin'."

"I'll be there at 10:30 then," he said with a smile. They both laughed.

~~~

After their first class, Seth ran into Dwight in the hall.

"So, Seth, give me an update on the newspaper. I hear good things through the grapevine, anyhow."

"Well, to tell you the truth, I'm starting to actually enjoy this a little bit, but what do you hear through the grapevine about me?"

Dwight laughed and pushed Seth on the shoulder.

"You do worry about what people think about you, don't you? And I always had you pegged for such an independent cuss."

"I don't need to stand here and take this abuse," Seth laughed.

Just then a tall, ruddy gentleman with a huge mustache in a blue uniform walked right up to Dwight and stood, waiting.

"Seth, you remember Gus Ford, the fireman from the assembly the other day? Gus is here for our quarterly fire inspection. Gus, this is one of Taft's truly unique specimens of humanity; Seth Knight."

Gus reached out his large hand and said, "Happy to meet you, Mr. Knight," with a voice so deep it seemed almost unreal.

"Nice to meet you too, sir, but I really need to be trotting along. I'd love to stand around and chat, Dwight, but some of us in this institution actually have work to do."

"Well, Seth, drop into my office real soon, okay?"

"Sure man!" Seth said over his shoulder as he headed down the hall.

~~~

With only two more football games in the regular season, even Seth was a little preoccupied that day with a whole list of new plays to finish learning by practice. Friday practices were usually short to save the team for the game, but coach Gazoni kept them an extra half hour this time. He wanted to win more than anybody on the team. In spite of the pressure of the upcoming game and the excitement of Halloween, Seth found himself thinking a lot about the arson case. He also found himself looking forward to meeting with the other three guys to exchange new information.

~~~

When it came time to be a football player that evening, however, Seth was 100% football and the Taft Bulldogs won the game by a wide margin. After the game, while most of the players were hooting it up in the locker room, Seth showered, dressed quickly, and slipped out the side door. As he walked alongside the industrial arts building towards the parking lot he was totally unaware of someone following him in the shadows. Seth ducked through the complex of buildings and emerged through a break in the hedge that surrounded the school on the far end of the parking lot. The skinny figure crept along the opposite side of the hedge. Seth stopped at his car which was parked in his usual spot in the far corner of the lot where the hedge was broken by a large tree. He paused by the door of his car and fumbled through his backpack for his car keys. The dark figure was only a few feet away from him and actually started to quietly push his way through the hedge when Travis swung around the corner with his father and yelled,

"Hey, hotdog! See you at the party!"

The person in the bushes froze. Bloodshot eyes glared out from the bushes at Seth with a look of hate and revenge.

"Sure thing, man! I'll spot you right off I bet!" Seth laughed.

"Five bucks!"

"You got it apeman!" This exchange gave Seth enough time to dig out his keys and unlock the door. His convertible started right up with a roar and he raced off, leaving the gaunt figure standing alone, watching Seth's tail lights disappear into the night.

CHAPTER NINE

Gunther and Travis both showed up at nine o'clock for breakfast the next morning. Seth cooked up a whole loaf of French toast and they all sat around the table eating and laughing as Seth told the story of the rat in the box and how scared Greg looked when he almost got caught in the bush.

"I guess we would have been hard pressed to explain what we were doing in the bushes with confidential records at 1 o'clock in the morning when good boys are supposed to be home in bed, but I know something would have come to mind. It always does. Did you have any trouble, Gunther?"

"No, not really."

Greg cut in on the conversation.

"I might be havin' trouble, Seth. Somebody been following me around after school. I knew it was important for nobody to know where I'm livin' so I always ditch the guy."

"Do you have any idea who it is that's following you?" Seth asked.

"No. I didn't know the guy, but I didn't see him too good neither. I think he's kinda young."

"Well..." Seth scratched his head thoughtfully.

"We have to make sure that these creeps don't find out where you are or they're likely to try and torch this place too. I don't know. Maybe we're getting a little paranoid. Are you sure someone was following you, Greg?"

"Uh-huh."

"I say set a trap for the kid and find out where he's coming from, Seth. It should be a cinch," Travis chimed in.

"That will be easy, Travis," Greg said with a big grin. "I'll just hide when he follows me and grab him when he comes by. Usually I'm trying to ditch the guy anyhow so he won't expect it. When I get him I'll just let Seth come and talk to him. I'm not too good at the talking part, but I can grab real good."

Seth pounded Greg on the back, laughing.

"Don't we all know, Greg. Don't we all know! That sounds like a good plan to me. We can do it on Monday, okay?"

"Sure, Seth."

"Well, let's get this thing going, guys. You bring those print-outs, Gunther?"

"Four copies, naturally." Gunther passed out his printouts, which were several pages in length.

"Wow! We got all this stuff already?" Travis asked, amazed at the amount of data in his hands.

"Sure! I actually didn't include everything that I got from the City files. The rest of it is still on the disk at home. This here is just the really vital stuff, Travis."

Seth interrupted.

"So! The fires here in town started just a few months after Wilson started working at Taft!"

"Yeah, Seth, and what's more, he came here from some high school in Chicago, which is the location of a number of the other fires. You'll notice that this file only has a general list of where the arsonist has been before, but no specific dates. Greg and I haven't been able to get in touch with the Ghost yet. I'd like to try and get some more information out of him. I'm sure that if we can't get what we need from him we can locate it somewhere else, Seth. We at least have some more..."

Travis interrupted Gunther.

"Seth, if the torch really is Wilson, we sure have made one big mistake."

"How's that, Travis?"

"Well, we did have him develop the film the other day you know. I guess that means he knows that we're interested in the fires downtown and he knows that we know about Butch. Who knows? Maybe the two of them are in it together? I can't see that Wilson had anything to do with Greg's house, but maybe someone else in Butch's gang did the job for them? What do you think?"

"I think that we should have someone else do our developing for now until we know for sure about Wilson. If we don't show up with any more film he may just let it pass. I guess there's nothing we can do about the past. I personally would like to go have a look at where Wilson lives and start watching him to see what we can find out. I also want to go straight to his house next time we hear about a fire and see if the buzzard is gone. If he's home, it would rule him out anyway. As far as someone else in Butch's gang doing Greg's house, I think that's a real good possibility, Travis, and once we get this Wilson thing more secure we should follow up on that angle too. What else do we got going here, guys?"

Greg spoke up.

"Seth, I think that maybe we shouldn't say nothin' about what I done to Butch."

"Good idea, Greg, but you can be sure that I'm going to let people know exactly what happened when this is all over. Now that you mention it, Greg, I think it might also be wise to leave the pictures of the downtown fires out of your article, Travis. What do you think?"

"Oh, I'm one step ahead of you there. The article is already written and I hardly mention anything at all in it about the fires downtown. We really have to work hard to cover our tracks, especially from my old man. If he had any idea what I was doing with you guys he'd go crazy. I just can't wait to see the look on his face when we solve this thing. He really thinks that kids aren't ever interested in constructive things unless they're forced into it. The guy doesn't have a clue, I swear."

Seth nodded slowly.

"Well, I guess the next step is to follow up on Wilson, and see if we can track down Strangerson for some more information about the torch's past."

"We should keep our ear glued to the scanner too, Seth." Travis added.

"Yeah, I think I will pay Mr. Wilson a little visit and check out the situation there. We all will be at the Chronicle meeting Monday so we can arrange something then if anything turns up. You know, Gunther, you should really make sure that you aren't being followed too, especially when you come over here. I'd rather not let a lot of people know that you are meeting with us on a regular basis. You're just too small, and too easy to squash. After the other day I doubt they would go after Greg with less than a battalion and I'm pretty sure that Travis and I can take care of ourselves. You got that?"

"Sure, Seth. I've already been making sure in my own way that nobody follows me. I've been small all my life so I have to protect myself any way I can. I'll be alright."

"Well, if nobody has anything else, I've got some work I need to do on my car and some work around the house that I've been putting off all week-"

Travis interrupted him.

"Hey wait just a minute! I almost forgot, Seth. You owe me five bucks from last night."

There was a huge grin on Travis' face as he held out his hand. Seth got a sheepish look on his face and dug into his pocket for the cash.

"So what's goin' on? How come you owe him five bucks?" Gunther squeaked.

"Oh I got suckered into a bet that I'd recognize him right off the bat and I didn't recognize him at all. Even after I talked to him for a few minutes. He was a fat grandmother. I swear, I thought he was a chaperone or something at first..."

After the boys chatted for a while longer, Gunther and Greg went up to the burned house to watch the workers cleaning up and Travis went home to type the final copy of his article, but deep inside all four of them, the wheels were turning all day long and a pride was growing that went beyond ordinary friendship. It was the pride of doing something worthwhile and belonging to something that was important. It was also a belief in each other. All four of them were seeing how important the others were and how impossible it would be to try and do the job alone. Seth was seeing this perhaps even more than the other three because he had tended to try and do things alone all his life and he was seeing first hand that one of his father's favorite axioms was really true. *'The two biggest by-products of independence are loneliness and mediocrity'.* He and Travis discussed it that evening as they huddled around the scanner.

CHAPTER TEN

The following Monday morning Travis showed up at the Chronicle staff meeting with a neatly typed article on trash can fires and one of the photos he'd taken of Butch and Rolly in front of the trash can. Ronnie started the meeting off with an attempt at roll call, but Seth cut it short.

"We're all here, man. Let's get this thing going, okay?"

"Uh, sure, Seth. Sure thing."

He fumbled in his briefcase for a bit, muttering to himself and then said

"First off, I want to welcome June Dunkinberger back to the chronicle and I'm glad we could work out the minor problems we had that caused her to leave in the first place..."

Marla Wexler poked Cathy Doherty in the ribs and winked as Ron droned on. They both glanced at June sitting at the head of the long table. She was indiscreetly staring at Seth. They knew the reason she was back. Ron continued.

"...anyway, the copy goes to the graphics place tonight, so I hope you all have your assignments ready."

Travis tossed his manuscript on a CD over to Ronny.

"Here's my article, Ron. I had Miss Beverly proof read it Friday so it should be okay. There's a picture on that disk too. Here's a copy of it. This is actually a candid shot of Butch Yorchenko and Rolly Howard lighting a can on fire by the Industrial Arts building last Monday but I don't think we should mention their names in the caption. Butch is still in jail, but that Rolly can be pretty nasty too."

Ronny looked at Travis' picture in awe.

"How'd you ever get this picture without getting caught? How'd you get this?"

"Good reporting, Ron, and who said I didn't get caught?" He glanced at Greg and winked. Annie interrupted.

"Here's my article on the drama department, Ronald. My father assures me that it's error free so you can save yourself the time. I certainly hope you find the space in this issue..."

"We need your article, okay? So don't bug me," Ron said, irritated.

"Fine. That's just fine with me, Ronald."

"I'll tell you what we need right away, guys, is money. We're supposed to be raising money for this paper to help it run, and June has been doing a great job of selling advertisements, but we also need to get the student body more excited about their own newspaper. Some of these people have never even read a single copy of the Chronicle yet so we need to come up with ideas that will get more people interested. Who's got some? Can anybody think of anything?"

Marla Wexler spoke right up.

"How about a bake sale?"

There were the usual groans and approvals and Ron cut them off.

"That's a stupid idea. We need something that more people would be interested in."

Jann Paris, usually quiet, surprised everyone by speaking up.

"How about a Christmas arts festival? Everyone in the community could bring their crafts and art and other homemade things to sell, and we could charge them a small commission. Sort of like a boutique. My mom goes to a boutique every year for Christmas and buys most of her presents. If we got started on the advertisement now it could be in the next issue in two weeks and-"

Ron interrupted.

"That's a fine idea, Jann, but I think we would really have to be advertising it now, and we don't have enough time. I'm sure we don't 'cause it's only three weeks 'til Thanksgiving, and we'd have to work up a theme, write advertisement copy, find photos and art work and-"

Seth cut him off short.

"Jann and I will take care of all that today Ronny. We'll have something ready after school so we can put it in this edition. I think this is the best idea I've heard of in a long time. It would be a great way to keep some of the big bucks that the Lake people spend on their Christmas presents right here in town, instead of going to all the big department stores. It would also help out a lot of kids and families in our school who can make nice things but don't have a lot of money to spend on presents. I know while Dad was in school things were tight and Mom said it got really old having to make shirts for Dad every Christmas. Is that alright with you, Jann? We can work it out in art class today."

"Sure, Seth. That sounds wonderful," Jann replied.

Ron cut in on the conversation.

"Well, fine. If you guys can do it, fine... I guess you're in charge. If you need any help I'm sure we can all pitch in and-"

"Ronny, Jann and I will need lots of help by the time this thing gets off the ground, but be assured that we will find all the help we need when we need it. I'm sure there are dozens of qualified people who would be glad to lend a hand. Even adults from the community who have experience with these things. That will serve the purpose of getting people interested in the paper, too. Don't worry, we'll take care of everything."

"Fine, then. I guess that solves that dilemma."

After a few minutes of general discussion the meeting was over. Seth strolled over to Gunther and said quietly,

"My place after school?"

"Excellent. I've got a bunch," Gunther replied.

"Ditto," said Seth as he strolled away and approached Travis who was still seated at the table.

"After school. My place?"

"Got it. News?" Travis inquired.

"Plenty."

"Great."

Nobody noticed the exchanges at all.

~~~

Later that day Seth encountered Jann just outside their art class.

"So what do we call this thing anyway, Jann?" Seth asked as they walked into the classroom together.

"I don't know, Seth. I haven't had a chance to give it much thought all day. There's just too much going on right now in math. Have you had any ideas?"

"Yeah. Ask Sylvia. She's brilliant at stuff like this. Maybe I shouldn't have volunteered us for this job Jann, I don't know. I just couldn't see a good idea like this go to waste. Y'know?"

"Well thanks for the support, Seth. This job on the paper hasn't turned out as interesting as I'd hoped at the beginning of the year. Ron kinda puts a damper on things, if you know what I mean. Anyway, why don't we talk to Miss Skondberg right away?"

"Sure!"

They both walked up to the front of the class to Sylvia, who was engaged in a conversation with another student.

"...and as I said before, your concepts are wonderful, but you still need some work on your basic drawing techniques to pull off something like this, Sally. Go to chapter 11 in the text and do a few of the exercises there, then do a series of sketches on the details of the piece to cement in your mind exactly what each object looks like. We'll take it from there. Okay?"

"Yes ma'am."

"My goodness, I'm popular today. Good afternoon, you two. You look as though you need help with something."

"It's like this Sylvia. Jann came up with this great idea at the chronicle meeting this morning..."

"I heard you were working with the paper, Seth. I couldn't believe it at first but I think it's a good idea. Now excuse me for interrupting. Jann had a good idea you say?"

"Yeah. Ronny was complaining that there isn't enough reader support and there is a general lack of funds. Jann thought of having an arts and crafts festival with the whole community involved, centered on a Christmas theme. Kind of like... well..."

"A boutique you mean?" Sylvia asked.

"Yeah. One of those."

Sylvia laughed.

"Have you ever been to a boutique, Seth?"

"Ah, no. Anyways we need help in coming up with a concept for it and some ideas for advertising. I sort of volunteered us both for the job of heading it up and we need the ad by this afternoon or it won't fly. The paper goes to the press today and it needs to be in this issue. Got any hot ideas?"

"As a matter of fact, Seth, I was thinking just last night of having some sort of a student art show. There are so many talented students in this class, and more people should be able to see their work, but this is even better. I'd love to get a lot of my Christmas shopping out of the way at a festival right here at school and I'm sure lots of other people would feel the same way. Let me get the class going and we can work on this in the back room, okay?"

A chill went down Seth's spine from the idea of being in the back room with Sylvia for the whole hour. His mind started wandering and creating a poem. Jann began speaking to him but his eyes were distant and he didn't respond.

"Seth! Are you all right?" Jann was poking him on the arm.

"Huh? Oh, I was just thinking... I have a few ideas I need to jot down real quick, okay?"

"Of course, Seth."

Seth always wrote poetic ideas down as soon as they came to him. He even kept a pad of paper beside his bed just in case. As he scribbled his poem down, Jann and Sylvia started discussing various ideas for themes for the festival. As Seth joined them they were tossing around a carnival theme as a possibility. Seth started humming Jingle Bells as he listened to the discussion go back and forth. Sylvia suddenly exclaimed,

"Oh! You know, that song reminds me of the sleigh ride in the snow last year. Did either of you two get to go on it?"

"Sleigh ride? Where?" Jann asked.

"Up at the mall. They must have had it there for a week. They had real reindeer too. Neither of you saw that? That's too bad. It was really cute."

"Hey! That might be a good idea to incorporate into our festival if we can. It sure would draw the people in, I bet," Jann said excitedly.

Seth was getting an idea.

"Wait a minute. How about...sure! How about a Charles Dickens theme? Then the reindeer and sleigh ride would be easy to fit in. We could get the drama people to dress up in old English costumes and talk with accents. We could sell tea and crumpets. We could get the madrigal group to sing. I'm sure Mrs. Bargar would be happy about that. How does that sound?"

Sylvia and Jann sat with open mouths.

"Seth, that idea is fantastic! What do you think Jann?"

"I think it sounds magical. That kind of artwork is my favorite and I love to do calligraphy too. It does sound like a lot of work. Who are we going to get to help us once we get this thing going?"

"There will be tons of people wanting to be involved. I think the main problem will be coordinating the volunteers, and deciding just where all the money goes. If we can get a few dozen people interested in bringing arts and crafts in from the community, we could be talking about several thousand dollars in commissions. I think that is a much larger fundraising event than Ronny had in mind this morning. What do you think, Sylvia?"

"I think you're right, Seth, but first things first. Let's get an advertisement ready for tonight and worry about the other details later."

The three of them dove in and came up with sketches and a clever description of what they thought the festival might actually look like. It kept flashing in Seth's mind that this festival was yet another way in which his life was changing. It all began the day he put out the trash can fire.

~~~

After football practice, Seth and Travis left the locker room to walk home. As they passed through the parking lot, neither of them noticed the person hidden in the hedge watching them as they set off down the street. The figure tailed them for a while, but when they turned to take the long way home he cursed under his breath as he headed off in the opposite direction.

CHAPTER ELEVEN

The afternoon meeting at Seth's house kicked into high gear at the front door, as soon as everyone arrived.

"First things first. Let's all go into the family room. Gunther, what have you found out?" Seth asked as he ushered them all in.

Gunther jabbered away as they walked through the house.

"Well, Greg and I had a long talk with the Ghost and several things turned up that are interesting. Take a look at your data sheets. According to Hike, our criminal is near the end of a cycle right now and getting ready to move on. He usually lasts two years or so in one place and he's been here for a little longer than that now. He announces his arrival in a town with a big fire then lays back for several months before lighting another. Then, the fires start slowly and build to sometimes three or four a month, and the guy disappears. Poof! At least the fires stop, anyhow.

I couldn't get too many specific dates, but Chicago was his last city for sure, which points to Mr. Wilson. The apparent date of arrival couldn't match any better because there was an early fire that isn't on our file here. Hike thought it was the guy's typical starter fire, and it was several months before any of these here. That would be just about the time that Mr. Wilson arrived in town. Hike also thought that the torch had a job that would allow him to transfer around the way he does without attracting attention. He even mentioned a teaching job as a possibility."

"And that's not all, guys," Seth interrupted. "I paid a little visit to Wilson's house last night and-"

"You broke in, Seth?" Greg grunted.

"No, I just sat outside and did a little spying with my binoculars. Travis, do you know that he made an enlargement of one of your pictures and it's hanging up in his living room?"

"Which one?" Travis asked.

"Let me see that first roll, Greg."

Greg opened up his battered briefcase and withdrew a stack of photos, spreading them out on the table.

"Here you go, Seth."

Seth looked at them for a moment and then pointed to the one photo with the crowd in the foreground that Travis had liked so much.

"It was this one, Travis. I didn't see much else in there but if we hear of a fire downtown and really race to Wilson's house, we should have absolutely no trouble in reaching it before he does unless he uses a long delay on his bombs or something. It's actually south of here. That's about all on Wilson, but Greg and I did a little strong-arm work on the way home today. It was a little seventh grader who was following Greg, and not too carefully either. Seems the poor kid was working for Butch, or at least that was what he said to us. I could tell the guy was scared. Right Greg?"

Greg giggled a little.

"Yup. He was shakin' when I grabbed him."

Seth continued.

"He said he didn't know why he was following Greg. Just that he was supposed to find out where he lives and report to Butch. When I mentioned that Butch was in jail, he just shrugged and said that he could report to any of the guys in the gang. Poor kid. Awful young to get mixed up with losers like those guys. Anyhow, I think that pretty much tells us that Butch was mixed up somehow in torching Greg's house. Now all we have to do is prove it."

Travis spoke up.

"You coming over tonight to listen to the scanner, Seth?"

"Sure. It's been a week since the last fire. Maybe we'll time it right tonight. I've got some work to do on the festival first, though. What time should I come over?"

"As soon as you can. How's that thing coming anyway?"

"Great. It's going to be a lot of fun. We have a Dickens theme with madrigals and a sleigh ride outside and all sorts of other atmospheric stuff, too. I think it will be fun for people even if they don't buy anything at all. I suppose I shouldn't have taken it on but Jann's idea was really good, you know?"

"Sure! I think you did the right thing."

Gunther broke in.

"Yeah, Seth. I thought her idea was great. If I was a little older, I would have volunteered myself. Leave it to Ronny to pooh-pooh an idea that could pull his paper out of the bog of mediocrity, you know?"

"Yeah, and leave it to the idiot to get all enthused about it when it starts looking great too," Seth added.

"Well Seth, I've gotta get home and work on math before my dad realizes I'm late again. I'll see you when you get there, huh?" Travis said.

"Sure! You want a ride?"

"Sure!"

"You too Gunther. C'mon Greg. Let's get going!"

~~~

It was 10:15 that evening when Travis finally called. Seth had gotten into planning the festival brochure and had lost track of time.

"Seth! A fire! Can you come over?"

"Be there in a minute!" He ran out to his car with his shoes in his hand and raced off towards the other side of town where Travis lived. As he pulled up to the front of Travis' house, Travis was waiting in front with his camera hung over his shoulder.

"Let's go to Wilson's house, okay?" Seth yelled out the car window.

"Yeah! Great idea!"

As they drove south on the highway to Mr. Wilson's house they discussed the possibilities of what to do if Mr. Wilson wasn't home.

"Tell me this, Seth. The lights are out and the shades are pulled. How will we decide if he's home or not?"

"Simple, Travis. Weren't you ever a rowdy kid before? We just pound on the door and run when the lights come on. No sweat."

They drove up and the shades were pulled and the lights were off, so they went up and knocked on the door for several minutes.

"You know, Travis, I'm a dummy, I swear."

Seth walked over to the garage door and pulled it up a little bit.

"Just as I thought. There's no car here. Let's go to the fire right now."

The scene of the fire was very busy by the time they got downtown. It was on the other side of the river in the industrial part of town and looked like an office complex. The two boys parked several blocks from the blaze and walked. As they rounded the corner and started approaching the smoldering building, Travis grabbed Seth's arm.

"Look! There by the hedge under that street light. Isn't that Mr. Wilson?"

Seth stared for several seconds. It was indeed, the industrial arts teacher from their school. He had a large parcel under his arm and stood, staring at the fire, completely unaware of the two boys across the street.

CHAPTER TWELVE

The Taft Chronicle came out on time Wednesday morning, and for the first time in several years, it was a big success. After it was in circulation for only a few hours it was hard to find a copy, and after a day and a half, it was impossible. The success of this issue was due, in part, to the new staff member from the football team and in part, to the great picture of Butch and Rolly on the front page. Everyone knew it was them, but very few people had the guts to talk about it in public. Needless to say, the trash can fires stopped. Everyone attributed this to the great article and photo by Travis. Travis was reflecting on this in his second period English class as Miss Tina Beverly went around the class collecting an assignment from the day before. She had put a list of five subjects on the board, handed out some paper and told everyone to write one page on the subject of their choice from the list on the blackboard, to be handed in the following day. Everyone had breathed a sigh of relief when she had said 'tomorrow'. Usually it was 'at the end of class today'.

Travis had chosen the first title on the list, because it was the easiest for him. It was loneliness, a subject that he knew a great deal about. The demands that his father usually made on him didn't leave much time in his life for friends. This year had been the first time in Travis' life that he had asserted himself around his father, and it had actually been the recent influence of Seth that had gotten him going. It was fun to have friends and to go out and do things together. Travis had never had as much fun in his life as he was having with the other three guys working on their fire project. Travis' dad had grown up by the sweat of his brow on a farm in Iowa, so he couldn't appreciate Travis' new desire for freedom. He had, over the last several days, responded to Travis' new 'attitude' as he called it, with silence and withdrawal. This was the central theme of Travis' paper.

As Tina collected the last of them, she went back to the front of the class and sat down at her desk.

"Today, we will have the unique opportunity to see inside each other's minds for a few moments. I am going to read all the papers that I have collected here today, unless someone has included something that he or she didn't want read aloud. If that is the case, please speak up now so I can set yours aside."

This approach was always the best one, because people were usually too embarrassed to say anything.

"If I run across any names in these papers, I will just shorten the name to a letter to help keep the authors anonymous. I want you all to listen, not as if you had to guess the identity of the author. Rather, as if you had only one chance to get to know this person and had to learn as much as possible from this paper. Grades will be given on attentiveness."

The first several papers were bland. Tina breezed through them in only a few minutes and the class settled into a trance of boredom. Then she started reading Travis' paper.

"For the longest time I constantly would blame my tremendous loneliness on my father and the unrealistic pressure he always put on me to perform and excel. It never left me any time to be myself and make friends..."

The ears were already perking up in the class. This sounded pretty honest. Most of the people were already wondering whose paper it might be, but Seth knew right away and tuned in to what the paper was saying.

"...any more though, I think I suffer from the same disease that almost everybody suffers from, almost all of the time; fear. My dad's strict attitude was an easy excuse for my loneliness for a long time, but my real problem has been that I am afraid..."

By the time Tina had finished reading Travis' paper, the classroom was as still as a morgue. Seth looked around like he always did and noticed right away that nobody else was looking around. The whole class was either staring straight ahead or else looking down at their desks. It was as if they had heard too much and couldn't stand to let anyone else know they felt the same way as the student who wrote the paper. They were all afraid. Travis looked over at Seth and they nodded to each other. It was safe that Seth knew. He was a friend you could trust.

~ ~ ~

After football, Seth drove Travis silently home for a meeting, both of them locked in separate spheres of thought. When they reached the house, Gunther and Greg were already there, quietly waiting in the living room. Seth relayed what had happened on Monday night.

"...and when we got there, Wilson was there standing in the shadows watching the whole thing. What he was doing there I have no idea, but we can certainly put two and two together-"

"Proof," Gunther interrupted. "Without hardcore proof we're nowhere. We need to catch him in the act or find fingerprints or something like that before we can go any further, and I think that we shouldn't work too hard to pin this on Wilson either. We might just pass up the real criminal in the process."

"You don't think Wilson is the one?" Seth asked.

"I think we should treat him as a suspect, Seth. That's all."

Seth scratched his head thoughtfully for a moment.

"I'll try and find out more about Wilson's background at school and we could match it with the info we get from Strangerson, if we can get any more from him. By the way, how are you two coming along with him?"

"I'm sure that The Ghost is good for at least one more session with Greg and I, so I'll give him a call-"

Greg interrupted.

"You got any new pictures, Travis?"

"As a matter of fact I took a whole roll and that also reminds me. Where are we going to get the film developed now? I'd hate to have to pay for every roll we shoot if this thing drags out very long. It could end up costing a fortune."

Seth replied thoughtfully.

"Yeah, I was thinking about that. I think I'll approach Wilson's teacher's aide for help. Tell him it's a surprise for Wilson or something and see how he responds. Other than that I can't think of anything, but I can't see why he wouldn't agree. By the way, Travis, your article was great. I noticed that the newspaper was pretty popular this time around too. It cracks me up how people are so afraid of Butch. Did you notice how people didn't want to talk too much about the picture?"

The discussion slowly digressed and Seth gave everyone a ride home.

CHAPTER THIRTEEN

The next day Butch showed up at school. He was obviously not too pleased with the photo of himself and Rolly on the cover of the newspaper and made it no secret that the persons responsible were going to be sorry that they stuck their noses in other people's business. Neither Travis nor Seth seemed to care much when people related the story to them. By the end of the day Butch actually was making a fool out of himself with what was generally believed to be an idle boast. It was not actually an idle boast for Butch. He fully intended to take care of both Travis and Seth. What he didn't reckon on was their newly formed friendship. He assumed that the incident with the burning trash can was a fluke and that it would be easy to find the two of them separately and teach them a lesson his way, one at a time.

~~~

After lunch, Seth dropped into the photography class to have a word with Armin Johnson, Mr. Wilson's aide.

"...and you see, Mr. Wilson seems to be real interested in the fires, so we thought we'd surprise him with a great enlargement of one of Travis' best pictures. You know, as a thank you for all he's done and helping Travis with his article. You think you could do that for us?"

"Yeah, sure Seth. I'd love to. I need some time in the darkroom anyway, so it would help us both out. Wilson's so pigheaded sometimes. Thinks he's the only one who can get the job done. I guess it's just his attention to detail or something."

Seth walked away from the short meeting feeling great.

After football practice, Butch and seven of his friends were standing around Seth's car in the parking lot, waiting. After Butch's bragging all day about how he was going to get even, Seth expected it and had a little plan of his own. Seth had to smile to himself as he rounded the corner and saw Butch and the gang as he had expected, but he acted surprised as he approached his car.

"So pretty boy, got a little carried away with your pictures, didn't you? I guess I'm going to have to show you just what happens to people who stick their noses in Butch's business-"

Seth interrupted.

"You just can't handle Butch's business without Butch's gang can you? I guess people are right when they say you're a stinking coward, although I hear you're great when it comes to intimidating little girls. I'll tell you what, son. Tell your meat-heads to back off and I'll show them just how much of a sissy their fearless leader really is. Maybe then some of these people can get on with their lives without being polluted by a jerk like you."

He stared with his piercing blue eyes one by one at the sad faces around Butch and every one of them looked away. Then Butch motioned for his gang to close in on Seth and they all spread out in a circle to surround him. Butch had a big grin on his face.

"You done preachin', pretty boy? You ready to get hurt?"

Travis' voice sounded from across the parking lot.

"If I were you, I'd back off right now."

Butch turned around with a growl, and saw Travis and Greg approaching from across the parking lot. The two of them jogged quickly across the lot and walked right up to stand next to Seth. Seth chuckled softly.

"Gosh, Batman, looks to me like you're not so eager to fight when the odds aren't seven to one. What's the matter, Butch? Cold feet? Don't like doing your own dirty work? Where's the old one-two, scumbag?"

Butch had to save face somehow, so he spoke up.

"You wanna face off alone, pretty boy? I'll tear you apart and you know it."

"I don't think that's the issue here, Butch. The issue is whether or not you're man enough to do your own dirty work, and that sure isn't something you're famous for. People aren't nearly as afraid of you as they are of your gang, Mr. Bad Guy. "

"You yellow, pretty boy? Lots of preaching but no action."

Travis responded with a smile.

"I wouldn't call being the highest rated receiver in the city 'no action'. You think you got enough nerve to face the likes of me on the football field, Nicky?"

This was the last straw. He sprung at Travis with a growl. Travis neatly sidestepped Butch at the last moment and stuck an iron fist into his stomach. Most people would have folded double from a blow like that but Butch felt no pain when he was angry. He whirled on Travis with a snarl of rage and like clockwork, his gang closed in on Seth for the kill. Travis switched into football player mode and charged Butch with a blood curdling yell. His massive right arm swung around Butch's chest and he threw Butch to the ground. Meanwhile, Greg had jumped in to help Seth and had tackled two of the gang and had them on the ground. Seth had placed a neat kick into the solar plexus of the first person to reach him and he had dropped like a stone.

There were four to take his place and Seth found himself overwhelmed. Something flashed in the sun and Seth instinctively threw up an arm to protect his face. He felt a sharp pain in his arm but there was no time to think of it. He reached out and grabbed a flailing wrist and slammed it against his knee 'til it snapped. There was a cry of pain. The weight of so many people dragged him to his knees, but he kept on striking out like a madman. Something scratched a hot scrape along his cheek, and his driving fist met the solidity of a skull with a sickening crunch.

He heard a yell behind him and felt a crushing blow to his lower back that just missed his kidneys, then another blow to his left shoulder that popped like a champagne cork and he ducked and rolled clear of the tangle of bodies just as a baseball bat hit the ground with a dull thud behind him.

Just then Greg literally dove into the pile of bodies on the ground screaming and started grabbing faces and bashing heads together. He had thrown the two others into the chain link fence and left them there stunned. Seth jumped for the one with the bat and wrapped his arms around his body, grappling him to the ground.

Up to this point Seth had been silent but the baseball bat was just too much for him to take. Already he could feel the angry bruises on his back and shoulder where the bat had hit him and he started yelling a wild scream and pounding his fist into the face of the attacker. Suddenly it was very quiet and two strong hands grabbed him from behind and jerked him to his feet.

"Seth! Stop!"

It was Travis. He had finally smashed Butch square in the face with a blow that would have stopped a charging bull and broke his jaw. Butch had dropped like a felled tree. Travis' left eye was already swollen and bruised and his shirt was torn down the front exposing an ugly cut on his chest from Butch's knife that bled a thin line of blood down through his chest hair to his navel and then past, soaking into the waistband of his pants. Greg stood with the shreds of several shirts in his hands, but had no marks on him at all. The sunlight suddenly seemed very bright to Seth and people were moving in slow motion. The fence behind seemed to dip and sway, and then everything went black.

The last thing Seth remembered seeing was Dwight running across the parking lot in slow motion.

~ ~ ~

The Taft Bulldogs didn't make it to the playoffs. With two of the starting players out of the game, the timing of the team was completely off, and a game they were expected to win was lost by two touchdowns. An issue more serious than the timing, however, was the morale; knowing that their two friends and teammates were unable to play made it very hard for the guys to concentrate. Unfortunately, Coach Gazoni couldn't understand this, and he lost his temper at halftime when the team wasn't ahead by a secure margin. He also lost the respect of most of his team.

CHAPTER FOURTEEN

Seth woke up with a start. The room he was in was dark and warm. It had a strange smell and he felt as if he had been run over by a train. He couldn't remember a thing. He heard regular breathing beside him and, for some reason, it took the edge off.

"Where am I?"

He wanted to speak out loud but it only came out a mumble. He tried again.

"Where am I?"

It was clearer this time, much to his relief, but the slow, steady breathing beside him continued unchecked. He tried to move but he felt as though he was tied down.

"Hey!"

It was supposed to be a shout, but came out a croak. The breather sputtered, groaned, and sat up. Seth could hear the sleeper fumbling around with the light and then 'click', the light cut into his head like a dagger.

"Owwww! What's going on? Where am I?"

Travis' voice cut in. "You're fine. You're in the hospital and don't make so much noise. I'm not supposed to be here-"

"What the hell am I doing in the hospital?"

"Well, four broken ribs, a separated left shoulder, about thirty stitches in your arm, some more in your face and a concussion to name a few things. The doctor told me you might not remember anything for a while."

"Remember what?"

"Well, you, me and Greg got jumped by Butch and seven other guys in his gang after school and we made mincemeat out of them, pal. I had my hands full with Butch. Greg and you took care of the rest of the gang."

"What do you mean we took care of the rest of the gang? What did we do?"

"I guess the worst thing was a nasty broken forearm. The guy's hand was bent back almost to his elbow. It was really ugly. Then there was the guys face that you rearranged. That was the guy who was beating you from behind with a baseball bat-"

"A what?"

"That's how you got your broken ribs and dislocated shoulder. This punk was pounding on you with a bat. He said you just turned around and grabbed him. Scared the crap out of him. He thought he'd put you out of commission for sure. I thought you were going to kill him or something. I'm glad I pulled you away from him or-"

"Hang on Travis. Why don't you start from the beginning-"

The door opened up and a nurse walked briskly in.

"I'm afraid you are going to have to leave young man. Visiting hours were over, ah, three hours ago. How are you feeling, Mr. Knight?"

"Like a plane wreck and I'm going to croak if you send my buddy away before I can find out what happened today."

The doctor walked in.

"And what may I ask are you doing here young man? Visiting hours were over a long time ago and-"

Seth cut him off. "Aw, doc, can't my brother stay for just a little while?"

The doctor looked at Seth with narrowed eyes, then broke into a grin.

"The name is Doctor Gordon Paris, Seth. I believe you know my daughter, Jann? I'm happy to meet you. I had no idea that Travis West was your brother. And after watching you guys play every week you would think-"

"Okay, doc. Can Travis stay long enough to tell me what happened?"

"Let me check you out first, son."

The doctor checked Seth over for several minutes.

"How do you feel Seth?"

"Other than sore and a little bewildered, I guess fine."

"Then I'd say there is a good chance you could go home tomorrow then, Seth. I'm going to have to keep you off your feet for several days because of the concussion and I'll want to see you on Monday morning at my office. It's going to be a while before you'll have full use of that arm again, Seth. A dislocation takes a long time to mend properly. I want you to keep the stitches dry, too. That was one heck of a slice. If you can keep it down to five minutes, Travis, I'll let you stay. You got that? Five minutes."

"No problem sir," Travis promised. Five minutes later, after a very thumbnail sketch of the fight from Travis' point of view, he kept to his word and went home.

~~~

Seth went home the next day, but wasn't able to return to school for almost a week. Travis would bring him his homework and a couple of friends came over to visit but for the most part his week was spent alone.

The one person who did spend a lot of time with Seth was Jann Paris. She came over daily so they could work on the art festival together and by the time Seth was ready to go back to school the following Thursday, a week after the fight, most of the conceptual work for the festival was done. They had organized a whole crew of people to help out with all the details and had started the planning for a Saturday work day when a bunch of students would go out and put flyers on every house in the neighborhood to advertise the upcoming festival.

Seth slid quietly into homeroom Thursday morning just before the bell and sat down next to Travis.

"Hey, Seth! Good to see you back! How's the shoulder?"

"Coming along a little too slow for me, Travis. How's things shaping up with, ah, you guys? I feel out of it, man."

"Oh, nothing new to date. I would've let you know if anything had come up." He leaned over close to Seth and whispered, "I went out last night and got some pictures. I should get 'em back tomorrow afternoon if you want to get together then."

"Yeah. Good idea. I feel like I been out for a month. By the way, the memory is slowly coming back, Travis. I've had some really interesting dreams the last few nights."

The teacher interrupted from the front of the class.

"I'd like to welcome Seth Knight back to school. I'm sure we all are glad to see he is okay. Right class?"

The classroom burst into applause for Seth, and the rest of the day went pretty much the same. Seth's favorite part of the day was when Sylvia Skondberg came up to him at lunch and, with genuine tears in her eyes, told him how worried she had been and planted a kiss on his forehead.

~~~

After school, Seth dropped into Dwight's office. Dwight and Tina were discussing what they were going to do the following evening, and Seth picked up on the gist of the conversation right away.

"Soooo, you two lovebirds are hitting the town tomorrow night, huh?"

"I'd poke you in the nose slimebag, but I can see that somebody beat me to it. As a matter of fact we were discussing dinner tomorrow night, and I hope you have the good sense to keep your mouth shut. I don't want people to get the wrong idea around here."

"Gee, Dwight, with all the lecturing you do to me about matters of the heart, it seems you need a little of the same medicine."

"Enough of this. How are you doing, Mr. Knight?" Tina interrupted.

"Oh, I guess I'll live a while yet, Miss Beverly."

"Well, we were really worried there for a while, Seth. When the ambulance took you away from here last week you looked awful-"

Dwight interrupted.

"Now what's the scoop on this Christmas festival, Seth? I've been hearing all sorts of reports about this, but none of it sounds too much like you. What's going on?"

"It doesn't sound like me because it isn't my idea, Dwight. It's Jann Paris' idea. I'm just helping her out. That's actually why I'm here man. I thought you could give me some input...." Seth briefly described what had happened with the festival up to then and how much work they had to do to be ready on time. True to form, Dwight came up with some great ideas for advertising and also offered to help round up some props from the local opera. The three of them chatted for a while and then Seth left, sensing that Tina wanted a little more time alone with Dwight before they left for the day. For some reason, Seth really enjoyed the two of them together.

CHAPTER FIFTEEN

The next day the guys got together after school. It was much the same as the other meetings before, sharing little tidbits of information they had collected and setting new goals for the future. Gunther so far had not been able to get in touch with Strangerson, so he hadn't been able to find out any more details about the torch's whereabouts before Chicago. Seth let the guys know that he was getting bogged down with plans for the festival, with less than three weeks to go, a work day the next day and a new ad for the paper the following week that hadn't been started yet. Plus there was all the school work he had fell behind in while he was out.

"Say, Seth, who are you taking to homecoming?" Travis asked out of the blue. Seth sat with an open mouth and a look of bewilderment for several moments.

"Don't tell me you forgot about it man!" Travis laughed. The sheepish look on Seth's face made the other three burst out laughing.

"Seth, I must of heard half a dozen girls talking and wondering who it was you were going to take. I bet it's the question of the hour right now," Travis chuckled.

"I ought to take Mom and make 'em all guess. Crap, Travis. I forgot all about it. What a dork I am. I really want to go, but don't you think it's a little late to be asking someone now? The dance is next Friday-"

Gunther interrupted.

"Personally, I'd say that for Seth Knight, the very definition of looks and charm, you could wait until next Thursday to ask someone and still not offend them one bit. In fact, you could probably take applications."

They all laughed uproariously at this and Seth cut in.

"Now come on, guys. This is a serious matter, and you happen to be totally full of crap, Gunther. I might not listen to another word you say for that last comment, unless you can come up with a good suggestion for someone for me to ask."

Gunther rolled his eyes and stood up with a grandiose gesture.

"Gentlemen of the jury, I bring before you the most exquisite example of womanhood and the obvious choice for a date for Mr. Knight here. The envelope please..... and the candidate is....Miss Sylvia Skondberg!"

The others responded with cheers but Seth groaned and put his head in his hands.

"No mercy. I get no mercy."

Greg spoke up softly.

"I think you should take Jann Paris, Seth. She isn't going and she is a real nice person, too."

Seth looked up at Greg with a look of astonishment and Travis chimed in.

"Great idea Greg! Whaddya think Seth?"

"Jann is the perfect idea. We've been having a blast the last week working on the festival together. Greg, put 'er there pal. Who are you taking?"

"Aw, Seth, nobody would want to go with me. That's okay though. I don't know how to dance anyhow."

"Well, what about you, Gunther? You going?"

"Naw. What about YOU Travis?"

"Sure am! I asked Roxanne Winter a month ago. I don't mess around with these things."

All three of them burst out in groans and hoots.

"ROXANNE WINTER!!!? How did you get her to go with you?"

"Hey guys, we've already gone out quite a few times and we hit it off real good. She's got a lot more than looks too, Seth. Did you know she has almost a 4.0? I'm talking serious subjects too. I've had my eye on her for over a year now. Ever since she broke up with Stan."

"That settles it then," Seth said, pacing back and forth.

"We're gonna find dates for these two right away! You got that? You guys are going if I have to teach you to dance myself. But first things first. I'd better call up Jann right now and reserve a spot on her calendar and then we can get down to some serious matchmaking...."

With the excitement of finding dates and talking about the dance, the subject of fires was completely forgotten for the time being.

Jann Paris was tongue-tied by Seth's offer when he called.

"...I'm sorry I called so late, Jann, but with the fight and everything I just forgot that homecoming was so close."

"That's okay, Seth."

"Well, how about we do some dinner first then?"

"Well, sure, Seth. I'm... I'm overwhelmed."

"Please don't be Jann. You know, it's been so much fun working with you on this festival, I guess you were the obvious choice for a grand evening on the town. So let's plan on too much fun, okay?"

"You mean you didn't.... well..." There was a long pause.

"Ask someone else first and get turned down?"

"Well... yeah. You mean you actually wanted to go with me?"

"No to the first and yes to the second. Don't make me out to be what everyone else does, Jann. It's been a long time since I've been out on a real date. I guess that whole scene just doesn't interest me much. I like having fun, and dates usually aren't. Everybody's always too nervous. You know what I mean?"

"As a matter of fact, Seth, yes I do but I've never heard anyone come right out and say it. Well if we're going to have fun, we'll have to match. Let's get together Monday at lunch and talk about what we're going to wear."

"You're on, woman! You bring the crackers and I'll bring the cheese!"

"Okay, Seth. Thanks for asking! Talk to you later!"

"Bye!" Seth hung up the phone with a giant grin on his face.

"Well shucks. That was easy as ho-in' taters! Hot dawggy!" Everybody laughed.

"Okay, Travis. You and I come up with some names, Greg will supply the phone numbers and we all can come up with an angle. Greg, first of all you gotta get a slick new hairdo, man. Then you gotta get a new set of threads for the occasion and you'll be all set. Got it?"

"Sure Seth."

"Well, let's retire into the family room so we can get some real work done."

The first three girls they called were already going to the dance, and the next one on the list was Marla Wexler, from the Chronicle staff. She had an incredible ability to talk, and Seth figured that between her mouth and Greg's memory they would have a good time. Marla wasn't a classically beautiful girl, but at least she was tall. You would have to be tall to dance with Greg. Seth did the talking on the phone.

"This is Seth Knight? Seth Knight from school?" Marla asked.

"Yes ma'am. I was wondering if you already had plans for the homecoming dance?"

"Well no, Seth. I, ah, don't right now."

An idea was forming in Seth's mind as he talked to Marla to help encourage her to try a date with Greg.

"Well, Jann and I are going to the dance together and-"

"You're taking Jann Paris?" Marla spurted out.

"Sure! And like I was saying, we were planning on going out to dinner before and maybe downtown afterwards too, you know, the whole nine yards. But one of my good buddies hasn't got anyone to go with yet and I was hoping you would enjoy our company for the evening. You know Travis West, don't you?"

"You mean Travis West needs someone to go with?"

By this time everybody knew what was going on and they were all jumping up and down cheering Seth on and trying not to make any noise at the same time.

"Oh no. He's going with Roxanne Winter, of course, and-"

"He's going with Roxanne Winter?!" Marla's voice was getting higher and higher by the minute.

"Of course they are. They've been seeing each other for a while now, and there'll be a few other people along too. You know. A regular entourage. It should be a blast Marla. A really cool time for us all. Are you at all interested?"

"Well you can bet I am, Seth! Sure! That sounds great! But, ah, who is it that needs a date?"

"Oh! Didn't I tell you hon? It's Greg Francovich! We're planning on having a fantastic time, Marla, and to tell you the truth, I'm really glad you're going to join the party. Kinda keep it under your hat that we're going out before hand so we don't get a lot of crashers. You know how everybody wants to show up when there's a party even if they're not invited? We'll all get together early next week and decide on where to go and what to wear, okay? We want to look outstanding together now, Marla. All right?"

"Uh, sure Seth. Sounds, uh, great. Thanks for calling me."

"Sure Marla. I'll see you Monday morning. Bye."

The four of them burst out in yells and applause as soon as Seth hung up the phone.

"I took certain liberties there Travis. I hope you don't mind."

"The idea was 100% inspired, Seth. Roxanne will flip over it. Just how much is this fiasco going to cost anyhow? I'm a man of very limited resources."

"If we need money, we'll get creative about raising it, that's all. Now, let's get a date for Hack-"

Greg interrupted.

"Seth, did she really want to go or did you trick her?"

There was a long pause, and Seth looked Greg right in the eye.

"I will be totally honest with you, Greg. First of all, you two will have such a great time you'll forget all about the phone call. It might not be love at first sight, but it will be a new friendship and that's what counts, Greg, and yes, trick might be a fairly accurate word to use, but if you don't trust me, I'll call her up right now and give her the chance to back out gracefully. What about it?"

Greg sat for a minute and thought carefully.

"That's okay, Seth. I guess you're right. It's just a new friendship."

"Excellent! Now Gunther, Gloria Bradey is definitely out of the question."

Gunther turned three shades of red and Seth licked his forefinger and drew an imaginary stroke in the air while everybody laughed.

"You have your dream girl and I have mine, Seth," Gunther said quietly.

Seth poked Gunther on the shoulder.

"You're alright, Gunther, for a shrimp. I have a much better idea anyway. If you promise to be nothing short of a perfect gentleman, I'll see if I can set you up with my sister, Stacy. If you can put up with going out with a seventh grader."

Gunther's mouth was hanging wide open.

"You mean the sister I met at breakfast the other day? The one who looks like a carbon copy of your mom? The one who could drive men mad with her beauty? You're kidding me, Seth, right? Don't this to me, Seth if you're kidding me. You're kidding aren't you?"

"I'll do what I can, Gunther. I can't guarantee anything, but I'll have you know that she already has asked about you several times."

Gunther blushed bright red once again.

"Oh, my.... oh wow." He toppled off of his chair with a huge grin on his face and started to giggle. Just then Stacy walked into the room.

"Oh, sorry, Seth. I didn't know you guys were in here."

"Don't leave, sis. I have a serious question for you."

Meanwhile Gunther had scrambled up from the floor and began to stare at Seth with terror in his wide eyes as though he were facing a firing squad. Seth ignored him and Travis started to choke with laughter.

"Let me be blunt, sis. How would you like to go to the homecoming dance with a friend of mine?"

"What friend of yours would want to take me to the dance, Seth, or are you just making fun of me again?"

"No, I'm serious, and the friend happens to be Gunther here. How 'bout it?"

She, too, turned instantly red to the collar and whirled around on her heel and said as she flew out of the room,

"Well, he can ask me himself if he wants to take me."

Gunther grabbed his neck and started choking himself.

"Aaaaah. Did you see that? What panache! What utter class! How could a geek like me ever go out with a veritable Helen of Troy? She'll scorn me! She'll taunt me with incredibly witty axioms and make me feel like mouse doo-doo. She'll-"

Stacy stuck her head in the door and interrupted Gunther's tirade.

"She'll say yes if you have enough nerve to ask, egg head."

Gunther responded instantly.

"Stacy, I'd count it an immeasurable joy if you would be my guest next Friday evening at the homecoming dance."

She smiled coyly and looked Gunther up and down for several seconds.

"Sure! If my dad says it's okay. I'll go ask-"

"Please allow me the privilege of asking your father's permission, ah, if you thought that would be appropriate."

"That's fine Gunther. He's out in the garage. Come on."

As they left, Gunther turned around with his mouth open wide and bit into his hand in a gesture of consternation and absolute glee.

"That does it guys. We're all going together!" Seth hooted.

CHAPTER SIXTEEN

The evening began at five o'clock, downtown on the water-front, at the Knights' favorite restaurant. It wasn't the fanciest place in town, but the food was great and so was the view. Seth and Jann had come with Gunther and Stacy in Seth's car and Travis and Roxanne had driven Greg and Marla in Travis' dad's car. Seth hadn't been too far wrong in his matchmaking with Greg and Marla either. When Greg came to the door to pick her up with his new haircut and charcoal grey suit she didn't recognize him at all.

"May I help you, sir?" she said.

"I'm Greg, Marla. I'm here to pick you up for dinner."

She was so surprised at the change she actually didn't say a word all the way downtown. She just sat still, listening to Roxanne and Travis talk about photography and sneaking in as many peeks at Greg as she could without staring. Marla slowly warmed up as the evening progressed and soon everybody was gabbing away. After dessert they strolled out to the walkway along the water's edge to look at the city lights and talk some more. It was cold and there was a large circle around the moon.

Gunther pointed and said, "That phenomenon is caused by the light passing through thin clouds of ice in the upper atmosphere... my gosh! What was that?"

Right across the street a flash and loud boom blew out the lower windows of a three-story office building.

"It's a fire, guys! Let's go!" They all raced across the street. By the time they got there the fire was blazing on the first floor. Travis was irate.

"Of all the times to be without the camera! What a

knucklehead I am!"

The three of them watched in awe as the fire raced to the second floor and then the third. As pressure built up in various rooms, windows would burst out and the ghostly orange light would erupt from the resulting void in long arms of devouring flames, leaping and grabbing at the side of the building like demons. Up on the third floor the fire touched off a massive explosion, and the whole corner of the building was ripped apart, debris flying everywhere. By this time there were several other people standing at the curb with the kids, and a wail of sirens sounded in the distance.

Greg poked Seth on the arm.

"Look, Seth. It's the fireman from school over there. Let's go talk to him." He pointed at a lone figure standing in the shadows across the street.

"Yeah, Greg. Maybe we can pick up some information. Put on the innocent act guys. Gunther, you ask all the questions like you do with Strangerson"

"Right, Seth," Gunther responded.

The girls got puzzled looks on their faces and felt as if they were being left out of something. Marla spoke up hesitantly.

"What, ahhh, what are you guys doing, anyhow? What do you mean by getting information, Seth?"

Seth reacted cool and distant as they crossed the street.

"To tell you the truth, Marla, we've been working on an article for the paper on the fires downtown. It's to follow up on Travis' article about the fires at school. Now, Ronny doesn't know about this, ladies, so let's make it our secret for now, okay? And I mean secret, Marla. We're really doing a thorough job of this, and I want it to be a complete surprise to everyone. Okay?"

"Sure, Seth. I won't breathe it to a soul. Oh! This is sooo exciting! I don't think I've ever done anything like this in my life. Look, Greg, I've got goosebumps I'm so excited!" Seth interrupted.

"Quiet now. Gunther, take over please."

Gunther immediately started in on a loud line of innocent chatter.

"Well, Seth, I think, if he's a real fireman, he might know something about this fire and I really want to talk to him and ask him some questions about the fire and what it's like to be a fireman and how they could ever put a fire like that out with just-"

"Listen, kid, I really don't think we should be bothering this man..."

They were just walking up to the fireman at this point, and Gunther erupted in his squeaky voice.

"Gee, mister, are you really a fireman? Do you know how the fire got started-" Seth interrupted again.

"I'm sorry to bother you, sir. My name is Seth Knight and I recognized you from Taft High School. My little cousin here wanted to meet you and ask you a few questions, if that's all right."

The fireman turned slowly to the kids as if just noticing them. He was perspiring and had a glazed look on his face. Then he snapped out of his trance and wiped his face off with the back of his hand.

"No problem, young man," he said in his startlingly deep voice. "I... I happen to know, ahhh... the owner of this building and I know it will be a tremendous blow to him when he learns of its destruction... How can I help you?" he said, staring off into the night.

Gunther spoke right up, playing the part to the hilt.

"Well, mister, how do you think the fire got started anyhow because we were standing over by the restaurant and we heard this boom and I saw this big flash and boy was I scared, you know? How do you put something like that out with just a hose anyhow, mister?"

The fireman stared at Gunther for a moment before he answered.

"I really couldn't tell you how it started, young man, and if you want to know how we put them out, I suggest that you watch the men over there."

He gestured at the fire truck that came roaring around the corner. Gunther grabbed the man's arm as he started walking away and pleaded,

"Gee, mister, do you think this was started by the guy who's been in the paper? Do you think he did it?"

The fireman looked down at Gunther with agitation.

"If you'll excuse me son, I really must be going." With that he turned and disappeared into the darkness of the night.

Gunther turned to Seth with a shrug.

"Sorry, Seth. I guess he wasn't in the mood for talking."

"That's okay, man. I never liked the guy anyhow."

The kids stood and watched the firemen work for a while and then Seth glanced down at his watch.

"Hey! Let's get out of here. We only have a half an hour to get to the dance."

The dance was a sensation. The band, Kidd Gloves, played great music all night long. By the second set, Greg was beginning to get the hang of dancing and Marla was having the time of her life with him. He actually got asked by several other girls to dance, but he always said no, and blushed. Gunther and Stacy were on the dance floor the whole night. It was actually the first time Gunther had ever been to a dance, but he was naturally coordinated and it came pretty easily. Seth on the other hand was usually a little reluctant to dance at first. He usually sat and listened to the band play for a long time, but Jann really didn't mind at all. By the end of the evening everyone was crowded on the dance floor and having the time of their lives. When Seth realized that the band was almost finished he went up to the leader and asked him how much they would charge to play another set.

"A hundred bucks will get you another set. You got that much on you?"

"Let me use your microphone and I'll get it, man."

Seth hopped up on stage and grabbed the microphone.

"How many of you people will cough up a dollar to hear Kidd Gloves play another set?"

The response was uproarious. The guitar player opened up his case and the money poured into it and the band really fired up this time, playing some of their own music as well as taking requests for songs they had done earlier. After that, people were starting to get worn out and the band played several soft, slow numbers to cap off the night. There weren't too many people who failed to notice Seth and Jann dancing and holding each other very close on the final songs. Afterwards, because the dance had lasted a lot longer than planned, Seth decided to drop Gunther and Stacy off at home. They took Stacy home first and Gunther walked her to the door.

"Thank you, Gunther. I had a great time with you tonight."

"So did I, Stacy. Do you promise to keep a secret if I tell you something?"

"Sure. What is it?"

"That was the first dance I've ever been to in my life. I didn't want to say anything at first because you might think I was a geek or something, but you sure seem like an okay person, even with that gorgeous exterior."

"Well, I am okay, Gunther, and you're a goon if you think that I'm gorgeous, but you can say it all you want to. It sounds nice coming from you."

"I don't know what it is about your family, Stacy. You guys all seem so... I don't know... so happy or something. You know what I mean?"

"Sure! We love each other, Gunther, especially Mom and Dad. That makes you feel real secure."

"Well, can I... well, call you sometime?"

"Call me anytime you want, Gunther."

She stood there looking at him right in the eyes until he had to look away.

"Is there anything wrong, Gunther?"

"Well... I was wondering if... well, I guess I wanted to, um..."

"If you don't, Gunther, Seth will torment you about it for days so you better get it over with. It's not that painful you know."

He leaned over and gently placed his lips on hers to kiss her, but the two of them were too close to laughing to be romantic. It started as a tiny little simultaneous sound resembling a giggle in both of their throats, developed into a tirade of uncontrolled laughter that lasted for several rounds and five minutes and finally quit long enough for them to get in one very sweet good night kiss, wrapped in each other's arms. Gunther floated back to the car and despite their best efforts at conversation, his only responses to Seth and Jann were sighs and grunts. Gunther was hopelessly in love.

After they dropped Gunther off, Seth asked Jann,

"You want to go somewhere, Jann?"

"Tell you the truth, Seth, I'm all worn out, but I would love to go home and make a cup of hot chocolate and sit by the fireplace if you want."

"That sounds great to me."

They rode to Jann's house in silence, each wrapped in their own thoughts and both feeling very comfortable being silent. They didn't speak until they were in front of a crackling fire, sipping hot chocolate. Jann broke the silence.

"Seth, are you really all that crazy about Sylvia or is it just a game you play to keep the girls away?"

He turned and scrutinized her with his bright eyes.

"Why would you ask that, Jann? About keeping the girls away?"

"Well... I think, under all that confidence you're afraid of girls, Seth. In fact, I get the feeling that nobody really knows what goes on in there. I've known you, or known of you since the fourth grade when you guys first moved here and I think I've seen more of Seth Knight in the last few weeks working on this festival that the previous nine years. I never thought I'd like you very much to tell you the truth, because almost all I knew about Seth Knight was the reputation. What I'm wondering now is, where did all that reputation stuff come from? Most of it isn't true. You don't really date, do you?"

"Now which of your questions should I answer first? No, I guess I don't date too much, and reputations just grow on their own I think." He shrugged and then looked straight into the fire.

"As far as Sylvia goes... I was pretty preoccupied with her but I guess the thing is more of a tradition with me now. You know... I still don't know if she even notices me at all."

"Let me clue you in then. When school first started this year, Sylvia had, how should I say it, a change of heart towards you. I'm not sure I'd call it falling in love but it sure was a bad crush. There isn't a girl in the school who doesn't know that. I'm surprised you didn't notice the first day."

There was a long silence as Seth pondered this bit of startling news.

"What are you feeling, Seth?"

"It wasn't too long ago that, uh, well if I had heard what you just said to me, I would have been...I guess I'm surprised I don't feel that way, Jann. Almost disappointed. After so long, too. Hmmmmm. I must say though, I am relieved. She actually isn't my kind of girl."

"Were you writing a poem for her the other day in art class?"

This time he was visibly shocked.

"Don't tell me that everyone in school knows I write poetry too, Jann. I'll never go back. Nobody knows I write poetry. I guess except for you now."

"That was a hunch. You know, women's intuition. Actually, it's just a matter of deduction too Seth. I've been in quite a few English classes with you over the years and you were always the best writer in every one of them."

He laughed and then turned his intense gaze on her once again.

"You! Little Jann Paris. Always the quiet one, but your eyes are never closed, are they?"

"No."

He studied her for a long time in the flickering light, her shoulder length brown hair pulled back in an elaborate braid and her dangling crystal earrings twirling and catching the fire light and splashing it all over the dimly lit walls like dancing fairies.

"Can I read your poems sometime, Seth?"

The question took his breath away as surely as a sharp blow to the stomach. He bored into her soft brown eyes looking for deceit and found none at all. There was only compassion and tenderness in her features, yet the answer to her question got stuck in his mouth like stones. She returned his gaze without a blink and the question remained in her eyes for what seemed like hours to Seth.

It was the first time in his life that anybody had gotten this far past his massive wall of defenses and actually gotten a glimpse of the shy, elusive boy inside, a boy who was desperately lonely for a friend and yet terribly afraid of people at the same time. Her soft eyes felt wonderful and terrible. Wonderful and terrible. He fought the poem that was forming in his mind, but Jann's question remained unanswered. The answer brought a tear to his eye, and he wanted to turn away and hide it but he knew it wouldn't do any good as the tear worked its way past his eye and ran down his cheek and dripped off his chin onto his clenched hands in his lap. The feeling of a tear on his face was foreign to Seth, and his one forefinger reached out to touch the tear moisture on the other hand. She saw this as well. Seth gave in to the inevitable and spit the stones out of his mouth.

"Okay."

Jann reached out a small, delicate hand and traced the path of the tear down Seth's cheek with her forefinger.

"More than anything else, Seth, I want to be your friend. You are a very special person that probably nobody knows at all. I'd sure like to know more."

His good arm reached out and, like a rehearsed dance, drew her close to him in the flickering red sphere of warmth.

They sat in silence for a long time and watched the logs turn to coals and the coals slowly shrink to ashes. Then they sat in the darkness, soaring on fledgling wings of new love and wrapped in each other's arms, content with the still silence of a sleepy but intense togetherness. The silence was broken by a dull buzzing sound from upstairs. Seth came to his senses and noticed a patch of royal blue sky outside the window. It was morning. They heard the buzzing stop as Jann's father turned off the alarm, and then they heard him get out of bed with a groan of displeasure.

"I'd better go, Jann." He looked at her pretty face and shining eyes and it felt wonderful to be alive and no longer alone. He drew her to him and kissed her softly.

"Thank you for a wonderful evening, Seth."

"I think I love you, Jann."

"I know I love you, Seth."

CHAPTER SEVENTEEN

When Seth got out to his car he glanced at his watch. It was 6:30 and the art festival work party was going to meet at 9:00 to pass out fliers. He drove home and immediately crawled into bed to take a quick nap. His alarm woke him up at 8:30 and without any hesitation he bounded out of bed, threw on some clothes and raced out of the house. He grabbed a quick muffin and cup of coffee at the bakery on his way to school and rolled into his usual parking spot at 8:48 with enough time to eat his breakfast and ponder the events of the night before. Part of him felt exuberant and part of him was terrified and the combination made him want to get really busy so he wouldn't have to think about it. By 9:10 most of the people were there waiting, but Jann had not arrived yet and Seth almost wanted her to stay at home. It was perhaps a fear that, here in broad daylight the magic of the dance, the music, and the fire light would be gone and he would be alone again.

The the people were gathered on the steps in front of the school chatting and munching on their own breakfasts. They were waiting for Seth to get everything organized, but he was by himself staring into the sky. Someone touched him softly from behind and a warm wave of relief spread over him before he even turned around.

"I thought you'd never get here-"

He stopped short. It was Sylvia. For some reason he felt afraid and uncomfortable.

"I think we should get this thing going, Seth," she crooned in her deep voice. He wondered how in the world he could ever have missed the attraction that was painted all over Sylvia's face. He actually felt a little embarrassed, but managed to cover it up with a rapid assessment of the crowd on the steps.

"Is everyone here, you think?"

"I'm surprised at how many people are here. I thought there wouldn't be half this many to tell you the truth."

The two of them walked over to the crowd and Seth began splitting the group up into teams. He and Jann had made a map of the town and divided it into small sections so each group could work on their own section.

"Once your group finishes your section you can just go home. I think we should get a real good response from this flyer, and please feel free to talk to anybody you run into and sign 'em up right there if you can. Remember, the first people to sign up get the best booths so tell them not to wait too long. We already have a number of booths spoken for, so don't forget to mention that. The success of this thing really depends on us today. This thing is happening in ten days! Now, we shouldn't have more than four people on each team or we won't get everything done today. I'll start with you guys over there."

Seth was purposefully taking his time to give Jann more time to show up. The feelings were starting to churn around in his stomach as he got closer and closer to getting everyone in groups because he didn't know what to do with Sylvia. Somehow he knew that there wouldn't be anybody left after he'd organized all the groups and he would have to go out alone with her. A few minutes later he handed out the last map to the last group and sent them on their way. He tried his best to appear nonchalant.

"Well... I guess it's just, uh, us. I saved the neighborhood over by the far end of the lake for me because I know there are a lot of artist types who live over there and I wanted to do some hardcore soliciting. I think a few of the professionals would be a great addition, don't you?"

"Whatever you say, hon. This is your baby, you know. I think you're doing a marvelous job of it too, Seth. I hope you know that."

"Uh, thanks. I guess we better get going. Do you mind if I stop at the bakery for something to eat first?"

"Oh, Seth, I think that's a great idea! I could use a little snack too now that you mention it. We do have all day to finish this and I'm certainly not in a hurry."

The knot in his stomach grew to a boulder. They walked out to the parking lot and as they approached the cars. Sylvia spoke up.

"Say, why don't we take my car, Seth?" He looked at the tiny sports car with apprehension.

"Uh, sure thing, Sylvia."

Sylvia looked at Seth with a little frown.

"Are you feeling okay, Seth? You seem a little distant today."

"To tell you the truth, Sylvia, I really don't, uh, well I guess I don't feel too good. I got in a little late last night from the dance and-"

"You know, Seth. I never did hear who it was you went with, or is that a little secret?" She smiled and leaned casually against her car.

Seth was totally relieved when he saw Jann's car come around the corner and stop in a far stall. Jann looked out of her car window at Seth and Sylvia and her mouth fell wide open. Seth knew that he had to do something instantly.

"As a matter of fact, I went with Jann Paris."

He turned quickly away and started heading for Jann's car.

"Hi Jann! I was hoping you would come!"

He didn't see the disappointed look on Sylvia's face as he left her behind. He opened Jann's car door.

"Please don't leave." was all he could say.

The look in his eyes and the tone of his voice told Jann everything she needed to know.

"You okay Seth?"

"I am now. Can you drive?"

"Sure." Seth turned to Sylvia and yelled.

"Let's go in Jann's car Sylvia. My car is running bad anyway and we can't all fit in yours. Is that alright with you?" She nodded and proceeded to lock up her car and walk over.

"What's wrong with your car, Seth?" Jann asked him.

"Nothing. Boy have I been blind. I'll tell you later. "

The day passed uneventfully. The three of them had lots of fun when the new relationship was noticed and the appropriate adjustments in attitude were made, although nothing was said about it all day.

When they pulled into the parking lot to drop Sylvia off at her car she sat silent for a moment in the back seat before she got out and then said,

"You two mind if I say something?"

Seth's heart leaped into his throat.

"It's me that should be doing the talking, Sylvia, only I'm not sure what to say to you."

"Seth... I think you two are wonderful. I really do. I also think that you are the most sensitive man I have ever met in my life, but since I'm by far the oldest one here I guess it's my responsibility to do the talking right now." She paused and gathered her thoughts for a moment.

"You and I have had a little game going, Seth, ever since I met you. A lot of the game was just make-believe and a lot of the game was real too, and the real parts would sometimes change on us. That just made the game a little more interesting I guess. I must admit too, that the real parts changed a lot for me this year. I guess I started enjoying the attention. I've never had it so good to tell you the truth. Any time I needed an ego boost I would just turn to Seth Knight and poof! I guess it was mostly just you, though. You are a real gem of a man and, if I just ignored the facts of life, like fifteen years difference and me being your teacher as well, it was a very nice fantasy. Well... the game caught up with me today, Seth, and maybe facing it hurts a little but I sure don't want to lose you as a friend over it and I sure hope that you feel the same way."

"Like it or not, Sylvia, you are stuck with me as a friend for life."

He leaned over the seat and gave her a squeeze with his one good arm and they all laughed. Sylvia got into her car and drove away and Seth and Jann sat in the front seat of her car in silence for several minutes.

"Am I pretty to you, Seth?"

Seth looked at her for a long time in silence. There was a genuine pleading in her eyes that couldn't be satisfied with anything less than a genuine answer, so he pulled a small notebook and pen out of his pocket and sat for a minute staring at the blank sheet of paper. An image started to emerge.

She is gentle,
Like the sound of snowflakes falling,
Comforting,
Like a candle in the darkness.
She is tender
Like the shadows cast by starlight,
She is pretty
Like a lonely cricket's song wrapped in blankets of
Soft, silver fog.

"Nobody has ever read any of my poetry before, Jann. I hope you don't laugh. I guess this is the only way I really know how to answer your question."

He handed her the scribbled poem and his heart pounded so hard on his rib cage it stung his still-mending bones. He stared out of the car window, too afraid to look at her reading his poem, yet dying to know if it meant anything to her. A soft sigh escaped Jann's inner being and she wrapped her arms around Seth's neck and squeezed until he gasped.

"That is the prettiest thing anybody has ever given to me, Seth. Thank you."

They sat in silence for a long time, thoroughly preoccupied by each other.

CHAPTER EIGHTEEN

It was Monday morning and everybody had too much to do and only three days in the week to complete things. Thanksgiving on Thursday of course meant a four-day weekend, which meant there were only four school days left before the festival. The festival was something that nobody had ever tried before, mainly because it involved so much planning and organization. Mrs. Bargar called extra rehearsals for the small madrigal group that was doing the singing, to be held after school. In return for the entertainment, the music department was going to get a share of the proceeds. The drama department was spending extra time in dialect coaching and doing some special readings as well. They decided to approach their roles as concession help and street people rather than performing an actual play. In exchange for their contribution, they too were getting a cut of the profit. The home economics department, in lieu of actually making costumes for which there was no time or money, opted to dig up, on their own time, a large number of antiques to "dress the place up" in exchange for a small cut. The wood shop had offered their services in making the booths and the art department was doing the decorating, also for a small share. Seth was also approached by the PE department with a tumbling exhibition, the brass ensemble, the science teacher with an exhibit on science and just about every other department in the school including the custodial staff. Most of them received indirect answers and some of them flat refusals. The festival was going to take place the week after Thanksgiving, from Tuesday to Friday night. Most of the set up was going to happen on Monday, and those involved were given special permission to miss all their classes that day. It had taken some persistent persuasion on Dwight's part before Mr. Moore would go for the passes. In the end it was the potential money that made up his mind as Dwight had on hand the financial figures of several local boutiques that had been operating for years. Mr. Moore was one of few people who had no faith in the idea and thought of it as '...a monstrous waste of time.' He told Seth, 'but if you people want to do this there is nothing I can do to stop you so go right ahead...'.

Dwight was glad that Mr. Moore was making such a plain and public stand against the boutique because he was sure it would be a big success.

Although Seth had gotten a large number of people to help out in many areas, he ended up being involved in almost everything from start to finish, right down to the layout of the gymnasium floor, and Jann was right there with him the whole time. Originally they had wanted to have several rows of booths laid out like streets, but it involved too much work so they ended up setting the booths up against the four walls and leaving the space in the center of the gym for customers, and the several wandering concession people, and a stage area for the street performers whom Dwight lined up through the opera. The city parks loaned them a number of old fashioned street lamps they had used for a Christmas display one year and the opera loaned them some backdrops to hang on the walls to get rid of the gymnasium look. At the last minute, looking at the floor with the basketball lines painted on it, Seth bought a dozen bales of hay with money from his own pocket and they tossed hay everywhere. It looked magnificent.

Opening night customers were mostly students, parents and all the teachers. Seth had wanted to don a costume and wander around as a performer but with so many last minute details to attend to he really didn't have the time, so he contented himself with just wandering around with Jann and talking to friends all evening. Seth had called some of the local television stations to see if they could do a story on it, but had gotten no answer, so he was surprised when the truck rolled up and the camera crew set up their equipment and started shooting.

The spot on the news was all they needed. Business picked up the second night as the word spread and by Friday night the place was packed all night long. On Friday, many of the people from the community sold everything and the festival actually started winding down an hour early because so many of the vendors had sold out and gone home. The festival had been a bigger success than anybody dreamed. They had sold, with four booths from students and twenty seven from the community, many thousands of dollars' worth of merchandise. Seth was just content to drive Jann home afterwards and sit in front of the fireplace for several hours, watch the coals, and listen to the wind in the trees outside. Images of burning buildings kept creeping into his drifting thoughts as they sat there and he couldn't help but wonder what was going to happen with the arson case and how he and the others would finally catch the criminal.

CHAPTER NINETEEN

"Travis!"

The call echoed through the empty locker hall. Travis, at the far end of the hall, saw Seth trotting towards him, so he crammed his books into the locker and slammed it shut. There was something urgent in Seth's tone of voice.

"Bad news, Travis. I just had a real interesting talk with Armin Johnson this morning. Wilson is the wrong man."

The news was a shock to Travis. So far there had been so much evidence against Mr. Wilson it was hard to believe he wasn't the criminal.

"How do you know?"

"Wilson was born and raised in Chicago, married there, and the only reason he left is because his wife died a few years ago. He'd been teaching at a high school in Chicago for years. It was the school both he and his wife graduated from. That's why he had to quit."

"Well what was he doing downtown at that one fire then?"

"I asked Armin the same question. He thought it was probably the photo club Wilson belongs to. I guess they meet at a lodge building down there. Armin told me that Wilson has his walls plastered with photographs, which explains why he has yours hanging up there. I just didn't see any of the other photographs from the street the other night. I feel stupid, man. I almost want to quit this right now. At any rate we need to get together with the guys and figure out what we're going to do from here."

"Leave it to me, Seth. I'll get the guys over to your house tonight, if that's okay with you."

"Sure. That's fine. I'll be home all night."

~ ~ ~

Later that night, Gunther sat at the game table in Seth's family room with his latest printout, while Greg sat across from him with his battered briefcase full of photographs. He was watching Seth as he paced back and forth like a nervous cat, almost muttering to himself. They were waiting for Travis.

"It seems as if we're overlooking something guys. I sure wish we could figure out what it was. We've been over all the possibilities but nothing is clicking. It isn't this way in the movies..."

Seth's thoughts were lost in the fire burning low in the fireplace. The hot coals seemed to dance with each other. The slow flicker of red flames licked at the edges of the fire-sculpted logs with a soft hiss and snap of sparks. Greg opened his battered briefcase, pulled out a stack of black and white photos and spread them out on the table in front of him. All three boys had a sour look on their face. Gunther looked up from his printout.

"It sure seemed like we were on the right track with Wilson. The guy fits the part so well. I guess it was too easy from the start. You can't expect breaks like that..." Their conversation was broken off by a soft knock at the back door. It was Travis. He came right in.

"I got here as soon as I could, Seth. My dad was on a rampage, again. About stacking firewood this time. That guy drives me nuts sometimes..."

"Travis, anytime you need help with stuff like that you need to call, man. That's what friends are for."

"Anyhow, I brought the new pictures. Here, Greg."

He tossed the envelope of prints onto Greg's stack on the table, and walked over to the fire with his hands outstretched.

"Gee, it's cold out there tonight. How about we play some pool and forget about fires for a while?"

Travis was discouraged, too. Seth absentmindedly walked over to the wall and took a cue down from the rack and started racking up the balls.

Greg was quietly scanning the new photographs with the blank look on his face that only came when he was memorizing. Gunther got up and headed for the phone.

"I'd better call Uncle Jonah. It's getting pretty late."

"If he wants you home, Hack, I'll give you a ride. It's too cold to walk tonight. Tell 'im we're playing pool."

Seth glanced over Greg's shoulder as he sorted through the new photographs. As Greg paused with one in his hand, Seth reached down and snatched it from Greg.

"Would you look at this. That fireman from school, what's his name Greg? The one we saw at the fire the night of the dance."

"Gus Ford."

"Yeah. Well here he is in this picture. I wonder why."

Greg looked up at Seth.

"Sure, Seth. He's in a lot of the pictures. Let me show you."

Greg got out several pictures from his briefcase and lined them up. Seth's mouth dropped open wide and he grabbed his head.

"My gosh! Travis! We got our man! Look at this! Gunther!"
The others crowded around and looked at the pictures with Seth.

"He's at half of the fires we've photographed guys, and re-member if you will how strange he acted the night of the dance. I didn't think too much of it then, but it sure makes a lot of sense to me now."

A sour look crossed Travis' face.

"Hold on just a minute. Why would a fireman be lighting the fires? That doesn't make any sense at all. I mean, listen to what you're saying!"

"On the other hand, Travis, why would this guy be at all these fires when he's off work? He's in street clothes in these pic-tures. How would he even know about the fires? I find it hard to believe that a guy who fights fires for a living would sit and listen to a police scanner on his days off so he could go and watch fires being put out. We gotta follow up on it, guys, and we gotta do it right away. What do you say?"

They all agreed with Seth.

"So, once again, we need to figure out what the first step is. Gunther, my brain isn't working right now. What do we do?"

"Same as with Wilson, Seth. What we need is proof. It seems that this guy would have to be off duty to accomplish this, so we hack our way into the City's computer and locate the work schedule for the fire department and check all the dates. If they all match up we go from there."

Fifteen minutes later the four boys were at Gunther's house, huddled around his computer watching him dialing his way, once again, into the city's computer. He whizzed past the security in a few seconds. He then called up the main menu and began scrolling through. They came to the payroll section.

"Anybody got a guess about which station he works at?" Gunther muttered. "The payroll is split up between all the different stations. I'd hate to have to scan each one, and I don't know one station number from the next, either."

He was continuing to scroll as he talked.

"Hold it! Look at this! 'GENPERSL.CTY'. The guy's name will be on that list I bet. It'll tell us where he works too." Gunther opened up the indicated file and scrolled to Gus Ford's name.

"Seth. Look! He's only been a fireman here for two and a half years! So far so good! Here's his personnel number Greg and... well why don't you just remember all this stuff. Station number 35. Okay, let's go back to the main menu. Got all this stuff, Greg?"

"Sure thing, Gunther."

Gunther went back to the main menu and scrolled to the payroll section, then found the file name for station 35. He then went straight to that file.

"Here's our man, guys. Greg, scan the dates of the fires and compare them to the dates when Gus was working. Any matches?"

There was a pause as Greg computed.

"No, Gunther."

"Are you sure?"

"Sure I'm sure."

"Seth, this is getting serious. What if this is the real guy? What are we going to do?"

"Nail him, Hack, and toss his carcass in prison where he belongs. Are there any fingerprints on file for the arson?"

"Our file just indicates that they have fingerprints in their possession."

"What we need to do then is collect a sample of this guy's fingerprints. Let me see. Greg do you remember if Gus was on duty tonight or not?"

Greg closed his eyes for a moment.

"Yeah he is, Seth. According to the schedule anyway."

"Okay then. We need to go downtown later, it's... 9:15 right now. Let's say around 12 or 1 o'clock tonight we go to station 35 and lift something that will have Gus Ford's fingerprints..."

Travis cut him off.

"Are you crazy, Seth? You want us to break into the fire station when there are people in it? You gotta be nuts."

"Do you have a better idea, Travis? I suppose we could go there in broad daylight and ask him for the prints or maybe try and trick the guy into touching something for us, but even if we could do that we would probably smear them or something in the process, and also run the risk of him finding out what we're doing. You know what a crazy jerk like this will do to cover his tracks? At least if I get caught breaking into the fire station I'll be safe from Gus with all the other firemen around."

"Whaddya mean, if *you* get caught? You plan on doing this alone or something?"

"Not the whole thing, no. Just the breaking-in part. You guys will be out in the car waiting for me. We sure can't all go sneaking in there, and since I have the most experience in this department, I think it's my job to do it. You agree?"

"Yeah, I guess so. What about you, Gunther?"

"Sure, Travis. I just hope Uncle Jonah will go for me staying up that late. He's kinda square, y'know."

Seth reassured him.

"Leave Uncle Jonah to me, Hack. You're spending the night

at my house tonight, and since tomorrow is Saturday, we can just tell him we're having an all-night monopoly tournament or something. Sound like a plan?"

"Well, sure, Seth!"

"How about you, Greg?"

"Sure, Seth."

"Well then, let's hit it guys!"

CHAPTER TWENTY

At 1:15 AM, Seth, dressed in black, hopped out of his car which was parked across the street from fire station number 35. They had been parked there for over an hour waiting for the last light to go out upstairs. Seth recapped his plans to the others.

"I'm going in by those back stairs. Hopefully the lock isn't too tough on that door or I'll wake everybody up before we get to first base. Now, if anything goes wrong, I want you guys to get the heck out of here and meet me on Fifth and Market. The parking lot with the alley behind it, okay? I can probably run out of here faster than they can get a car going. I'll make for that fence across the street, and then over to Fifth through the alley. I might be able to get there before you if we leave at the same time, but I don't want to have to sit around waiting too long for you either, okay? Now don't forget, Travis, it floods real easily so don't pump on the gas! It won't start if you do. Just turn the key and it fires right up. You got that?"

"Yeah. You gonna be alright with the arm and all?"

"No sweat, Travis. The only time it hurts is when I use it, so I just won't use it!"

"Give 'em what they deserve, Seth."

They were all proud and scared as they watched their friend silently cross the street and disappear into the shadows.

Seth had been hoping that the back door led into a hallway, but it actually opened into the bunkhouse where all the firemen slept. Firemen have a reputation for being light sleepers so Seth had no room for a slip up this time. He padded up the stairs and paused at the top to catch his breath and nerves. Luckily for him, the back door wasn't locked. The street light was situated so the doorway was in shadow. No light would shine in the door when Seth opened it. He had to time it so a breeze didn't blow in when he opened the door, as the air was cold outside and likely to awaken someone. He also had to gamble that nobody's bunk would be too close to the door, and that there would be enough light to see what he was looking for.

After he allowed enough time for his eyes to adjust to the darkness, he slipped the door open and stepped inside. It was a large room with twenty or more bunks in it, although only half were occupied. There were several night lights spaced out on the walls that dimly lit the room, casting enough light for Seth to see.

Seth quickly moved to the first bunk, but the occupant was turned over. Then he went to the next. It was the wrong man. He continued around the room from bunk to bunk until he reached the one containing a large man with red hair. It was Gus Ford. His bunk just happened to be the one closest to the door. A smile played on Seth's face as he turned to open the chest at the foot of the bunk. Seth was looking for anything personal that wouldn't have been handled by anyone else, and Gus' electric shaver sat in a tray in the lid of the chest. Perfect. Seth pulled a plastic bag out of his jacket, gently picked up the shaver by the cord and deposited it in the plastic bag. Just as he sealed the top of the bag, the fire alarm went off downstairs and the lights came on in the bunkhouse.

~ ~ ~

Outside in the car, the others had been waiting for Seth to return. For the first several minutes they hadn't said a word and then Gunther broke the silence.

"So, Travis, how are we going to utilize the fingerprints when we get them, and how are we going to get the fingerprints off of whatever it is Seth gets up there, anyway?"

"I suppose we'll just take them to the police, Gunther, but I think I'd feel kinda stupid if I were to walk into the police station and ask them to check a hair brush or whatever for fingerprints because they might belong to the downtown arsonist. You know what I mean? That part we're going to have to leave to Seth. I suppose if he can pull off that poet thing at City High that Dwight was telling us about, he can figure out what to say when the time comes to close this deal. You know, we probably won't know for positive that this is the guy until we get an expert to analyze the fingerprints, although I'd put money on it now."

Travis was interrupted by the sound of the alarm going off and the lights went on upstairs in the bunkhouse. Gunther's voice squeaked with panic,

"Quick, Travis! Start the car! Let's get out of here!"

Unfortunately, Travis forgot Seth's instructions and pumped the gas before he started the car so it was flooded and wouldn't start. He cranked it and cranked it but all it did was turn over and start to wear the battery down. It looked like all their plans were backfiring on them.

~~~

When the lights came on in the bunkhouse, Seth realized that he had to move fast, but unfortunately for him Gus was a very light sleeper and woke up the moment the alarm went off. What he saw standing at the foot of his bed was a figure dressed in black with his shaver in a plastic bag, and it didn't take him but half a second to figure out what was going on.

Gus flew out of his bunk. Seth banged his way out the door with his bad arm and sprinted down the stairs, just beyond the grasp of Gus' clutching fingers. Gus began following Seth down the stairs, but the energy of youth was on Seth's side. He disappeared into the night, leaving a bewildered Gus at the foot of the stairs glaring and muttering into the blackness. As Gus returned to the bunkhouse, Seth ran across the street to his car where he was met with panic. Travis was still trying to start the car.

"Move over! Quick! I'll get this thing going."

This was actually easier said than done. Gunther was moaning.

"Oh why did I let you guys talk me into going along! I know

we're going to get arrested and thrown in jail, and I'm going to be on restriction for the rest of the year..."

"Gunther, would you shut up!" Seth scolded.

"...And Uncle Jonah won't ever let me out of his sight again even to go out on a date..."

"Gunther if you don't shut up I'm going to choke you!"

"...And I know it doesn't matter to you, Seth, because you get all the dates you want so why should I even bother telling anybody-"

"SHUT UP SHRIMP!!!"

Seth delivered this last directive within an inch of Gunther's nose by leaning over the seat. It finally got Gunther quiet. He easily started the car, but their troubles weren't over. Just as Seth put the car into gear the fire station car came squealing out of the station with the ladder truck close behind. Gus was at the wheel of the car, and as he backed across the street out of the station to let the ladder truck out, he pulled right out next to Seth's car, looked across, and recognized Seth as the bandit. Seth didn't lose his head for a second. He jammed it into reverse, backed up on the sidewalk, and roared off in the opposite direction.

Something in Gus' mind snapped. He floored it and squealed in a lopsided U-turn with the tires smoking and took off after Seth, barely missing the front of the approaching fire truck. The driver of the fire truck saw the red fire station car go racing off into the night so he naturally followed with sirens blaring. Travis yelled over the roar of the engine and the scream of the sirens.

"What's going on, Seth? What are we doing? How are we going to get out of this one?"

"The first thing we need to do is relax and think guys. Obviously, Gus is the man, so all we have to do is take the shaver I got-"

"You got it?!!"

"Of course! Now all we have to do is take this thing... look at this guy behind us. I think he's gone crazy!"

Gus was weaving all over the road behind them trying to get in front of Seth's car.

"Well, Seth, what do we do if Gus isn't the criminal?" Gunther whined. "He might just be really mad at you for stealing his shaver and-"

"Gunther, Gus is the torch. He's trying to run us off the road-"

Gus' car rammed them from behind. They all yelled at once and Seth stomped on the gas.

"Think for me, guys! I gotta drive! Gunther! Turn on the brain!"

Gunther grabbed his head and started moaning.

"Oooooh! Think! Think! What do we do? What do we do?"

"Lose him, Seth! Can't you lose him?" Travis yelled out.

"No. That car has more beef than mine. It's all I can do to keep in front of him, man."

Gus' car roared in a smoking arc as they both squealed around a corner, and then slid alongside Seth's car. Over the loud roar of the motors the boys could hear Gus's deep voice screaming at them and his bright eyes were red with hatred. Seth slammed on the brakes and Gus's car shot ahead of theirs.

They had lost the fire engine several blocks back but suddenly it skid around the corner and missed the rear of Seth's car by inches. Seth jammed the car into reverse and spun around the other way, tires smoking. Then he made a hard left turn the wrong way down a one way street and Gus' car was nowhere to be seen. The boys let out a whoop of delight, but as they zipped through the next intersection his red car was sitting at the corner waiting to turn. He took off after them with burning tires. Suddenly Greg yelled out.

"Seth! I got it! Lead him to the police station! Make him follow us to the Lake Oswego police so we can turn him in!"

All of the others erupted in a scream of jubilation and started pounding Greg on the back, but Seth suddenly snapped into a sort of trance of grim determination. His jaw was rigid and his forehead was furrowed with concentration but his hands held the steering wheel lightly, and he reached down and slipped a CD into his stereo and turned it up. Now that they had come up with a plan he was the cool Seth Knight that his friends were more familiar with. He began thinking out loud.

"I can't get on the highway south, or Gus will run us off the road. I'm going to have to go up over the hill to get down to Lake Oswego-" Travis cut him off.

"Seth, you can't go that way. The road is closed because of that new sewer line going in."

Seth thought for a moment.

"I guess we'll have to risk the highway then, guys."

Seth continued to weave in and out of the streets downtown, always choosing the streets that would lead them closer to the main highway south that led down to Lake Oswego. Finally, as Seth squealed around the ramp that emptied onto the highway south, a frown creased his forehead, sweat ran down his face, and his jaw worked in knots of tension.

"I think we'll make it, guys. I think we can do it. Gus is a ways back there and if I can just keep some distance between us for the next five minutes we'll make it."

"How's the arm, Seth?" Travis asked him quietly.

"Killing me, man. I smashed it into the door when I ran out of the fire station. I'll be OK."

Seth was cut off by a distant bang and a crunching sound in the back of the car. Seth screamed out at the top of his voice,

"Get down guys. He's got a gun!"

There was another bang, the rear window exploded into shrapnel, and the three passengers hit the floor instantly.

"Everybody okay?" Seth yelled.

"Yeah! Sure!" Seth began thinking out loud again.

"I think we should stop and scatter. There are a lot of trees-"

"He's got a gun Seth. We can't stop!"

"What if he hits the gas tank Travis? We're sitting ducks in this car man."

Nobody had a solution to that problem. Seth kept his foot to the floor and the two cars flew down the highway, but Gus' car steadily continued to gain on them. An occasional streetlight shot by in a blur but the highway was deserted except for the two cars zooming along in a death race. When Gus' car was only a few dozen yards away from Seth's car he yelled out,

"Get ready to run for it guys! I'm going to stop real fast. Head for the trees and scatter!"

He slammed on the brakes and slid his car to the opposite side of the road. As Seth's car skidded to a smoking stop, Gus' car flew past them before he could hit his own brakes and squeal to a stop some fifty yards ahead of Seth's car. Gus kicked the door open and jumped out of the car. He ran to the rear of the car and with a blood curdling yell, squatted down and opened fire on Seth's car which was sitting at an odd angle on the shoulder of the road. In the distance was a scream of sirens but Gus emptied his weapon at Seth's car, unaware of anything else around him. The last bullet found the gas tank and the car erupted in an ear shattering explosion and a massive ball of flames. The gun dropped from Gus's fingers as he groaned with pleasure at the sight of the burning car.

A few moments later, a Portland City police car skid to an awkward stop just behind Gus's car and the young officer jumped out of his car.

"Excuse me sir, I just got a report on the radio-"

He was cut short by Gus turning and jumping on him with a loud scream. Gus wrapped his massive fingers around the officer's neck and squeezed and shook with a vise grip. The officer, caught off guard, was helpless in the demonic grip of the fireman. Suddenly a shadow darted across the road and a huge arm slammed into Gus's head, knocking him down and away from the stunned officer. The policeman dropped to the ground with a moan and lay there in a heap. It was Travis who had jumped from the shadows on the side of the road, and Gus jumped to his feet with a snarl of rage and dove at Travis, catching him just around the ankle and toppling him, but Travis' football instinct was too strong and he rolled over once, twisting his foot free from Gus's grip and snapping to his feet all in one fluid move. Travis swung a tremendous kick into the rib cage of Gus as the man rolled to get up, and danced out of the way of Gus's hand as it swung around to grab his foot. Gus's breath heaved out of him and he paused for a moment on the ground in pain. Suddenly he rolled away from

Travis, snatched his revolver from the ground by his car and leveled it at him.

"You're dead kid. You're dead!"

A foot from the darkness connected with the gun in his hand, flipping it out of his grasp and away into the night. Greg grabbed Gus with a grunt, lifted him up by the shirt, and cracked him on the forehead with a head-butt that thumped like a rubber mallet. Gus groaned and slumped to the ground, unconscious.

"Where'd you learn that move, Greg? Looks like it hurt an awful lot."

"TV wrestling," Greg said, rubbing his forehead with a grimace. "Ow. It does hurt. You okay, Travis?"

"Sure. Let's check on this policeman real quick. Hey Seth! Gunther! You guys all right?"

Seth and Gunther stepped out of the shadows. Seth was staring bleakly at his car. It was almost invisible in a curtain of flames and the column of black smoke. The other three boys were huddled around the police officer, trying to revive him, when two Lake Oswego squad cars roared up from the south and screeched to a halt. A lieutenant jumped out of the first car and with a swift glance at the situation, barked out an order.

"Okay, kids, party's over. I want hands in the air and no monkey business. John, get a fire truck here for that mess over there and call in some backup while you're at it."

The lieutenant, officer Biggs, finally recognized Seth.

"I should have known it! Seth Knight! Well, I knew you were a troublemaker mister Knight, but I had no idea that you'd pull a stunt like this one. Now get over there with the rest of those kids."

He glanced at Gus, who was rubbing his head where Greg had butted him and slowly getting to his feet.

"Maybe I can get some straight answers from the fireman over there. Not a word from you, mister Knight."

Just then the officer on the ground moaned and opened his eyes. Lieutenant Biggs glanced down at him.

"You okay, trooper?"

"Yeah. Watch out for the fireman. He tried to kill me," he

rasped quickly.

Lieutenant Biggs looked warily at Gus and said, "You stay put for now, sir. I want to get to the bottom of this."

Gus, seeing Seth standing by the squad car let out a growl and jumped at him. Lieutenant Biggs' gun blasted the night air and Gus stopped in his tracks.

"I said stay put, or the next one will be for *you*, mister! Get your hands on your head. NOW! Let's cuff him, John."

He looked hard at Seth.

"You better have a real good story this time pal. I mean a prize winner or you're in real hot water. You and all your friends here."

Just then the scream of the fire truck siren was heard approaching in the distance as the two police officers put Gus in the back of the second patrol car. As a fire truck skid to a stop and the firemen jumped out to attend to the burning car, Travis leaned over to Seth and whispered,

"What do we do now, Seth?"

"Play it by ear for now Travis. I don't think the shaver will do us much good, but I also don't think we'll need it. I just need a few minutes to think. I'm still shaking and my arm is killing me. You two okay?"

Gunther and Greg were both pale with fear, but they managed an affirmative nod to Seth. Just then, two more squad cars pulled up and Lieutenant Biggs opened the doors of his car and motioned for the boys to get in.

"John, you can stick around here and get everything squared away. I'm taking these guys down to the station." He turned to the Portland police officer, still on the ground. "You okay?"

"Yes sir, thank you," the man answered.

"Well, the name is Biggs, and I'm anxious to get to the bottom of this so I sure would appreciate your help."

"My name is Paulson, sir and I'd be happy to do whatever you need me to do."

"Great. If you make your way down to the main station in

Lake Oswego that would be great. I'll need you to give a statement, okay?"

"Yes sir. Of course."

They all drove off into the night.

~ ~ ~

Fifteen minutes later, the boys were seated in Lieutenant Biggs's office, who stood in front of them with a scowl.

"Okay, guys. What's going on?"

Seth stood up and rubbed his face with a sigh.

"We're all pretty shook up sir, but the situation is actually real simple. That fireman you got out there is the arsonist from all the downtown fires and we want to put him under citizen's arrest. I really don't know how-"

Lieutenant Biggs interrupted.

"You want to place a fireman under arrest for being an arsonist? What? You think I'm stupid or something? What I want from you are answers and not any of this nonsense about-"

Seth interrupted the policeman with a stern voice.

"Do we or do we not have the right, as citizens of the United States, to put this man under citizen's arrest?"

Lieutenant Biggs looked at Seth, first with a flash of complete surprise, followed by a scowl that passed across his face.

"Fine, Seth. Just fine. But you're on your own, son. I'll need hardcore evidence for this charge, Seth, 'cause if you're not right about it, I will see you and all your friends in jail tonight. You got that? Jail."

Seth was not intimidated in the least.

"You want evidence sir? How about fingerprints? How about photographs? We got it all. You check your files for the criminal's fingerprints and then compare them to Gus's for starters, and if you need more than that, we have photographs of this jerk at the scene of all kinds of fires when he's not even on duty. Plus he was shooting at us, he blew up my car and would have killed that policeman if we hadn't stopped him. Yeah, we got all the evidence we need."

"We'll see if you're telling the truth soon enough Seth." Lieutenant Biggs replied with a grim look on his face. "Meanwhile you boys will need to stay here at the station until we can sort this out."

~~~

Needless to say, the prints matched, Gus Ford got locked up, and the guys were on their way to being heroes. It was turning out to be a good night after all. About two hours later, as the last of the reports were being finished, Greg was on a chair snoring and slumped over like a wilted plant and Gunther was asleep beside him. Seth and Travis were chatting with an officer in the front lobby. Hike Strangerson came bursting through the door with Rolly Howard in front of him in pajamas and handcuffs. He stared at Seth for a second with his strange eyes and then pushed Rolly forward to the front desk.

"Book 'im. Arson. He's the one lit the Francovich place. Say boy, whaddya doin' here at this hour?"

This last question was directed at Seth who motioned to Travis to wake up the other two. Then he walked up to Hike and spoke to him face to face.

"First of all pal, my name is Seth, or maybe you can just call me Mr. Knight if you can't remember Seth. As to your question, my friends and I have apprehended the real arsonist in this town tonight, and we were just wrapping up the reports now. If you're interested in who it really was that you've been chasing around the country the last few years, the whole story will be in the paper in the morning, and by the way, thanks for picking up ol' Rolly for us. Saved us a lot of trouble. What? Fingerprints on the bottles? Brilliant deduction. Let's go guys."

He spun around on his heels and they all marched out of the station with grim looks on their faces, but as soon as they were outside the door, Seth began to laugh. The others soon joined him as the events of the night finally began to sink in. Suddenly, Seth stopped short.

"Hey! How are we gonna get home?"

They all stopped laughing. Everyone was tired to the bone and this was no laughing matter. Just then, Officer Paulson from the city came out through the front door and saw the four boys standing there with bewildered looks on their faces.

"Hey you guys! I never got a chance to thank you for jumping in and helping me out before. I swear, that maniac would have killed me if you guys didn't do something."

He extended his hand to Travis with a big smile.

"If there's ever anything I can do for any of you guys, just let me know."

Greg smiled and asked,

"Well, how about a ride home? Gus blew up Seth's car."

"I'd be happy to! By the way, my name is Roger. Roger Paulson. So that was your car, huh? I'd love to know how you guys were able to track the guy down when so many police departments and detectives across the country had no luck at all."

Seth beamed.

"Teamwork! It's the only way. Right guys?"

They all nodded in agreement.

"Other than that, Roger, there isn't a lot more we can say about our operation. I'm sure you can understand that, right?"

Roger looked at Seth with a sly grin.

"You guys are pretty smart, I guess. Pretty smart. I'm really glad you're on our side. Why don't we get you home? It is getting pretty late..."

They all walked off towards the policeman's car chatting and laughing, but Seth remained quiet and withdrawn, the image of his car in flames still fresh in his mind.

CHAPTER TWENTY ONE

An elated group of friends gathered in the dining room at Seth's house the next morning. As soon as Seth had gotten home the night before, he had risked the wrath of Dr. Paris and called Jann on the phone and told her what had happened. Then he woke up his dad and told him, and they decided right then to have everybody over for brunch the next morning and talk it all out. It ended up being quite an affair. Marla came over with Greg and his folks, Seth picked up Jann, and Travis somehow managed to talk Roxanne into coming at the last minute, although she didn't feel at home for the first half hour until Seth's mom asked her for help in the kitchen, mainly to get her a little more involved. By the time the meal was over, everybody was having a great time.

Gene suddenly popped out of his chair and spoke out.

"All right, everybody, I think it's high time that we get the scoop on what has happened here the last several months and what these characters have been doing at all hours of the night. Who is going to be the storyteller, Seth?"

Everyone laughed as Seth rose solemnly from his chair and cleared his throat and placed his fingertips on his forehead in mock concentration.

"The actual chain of events began in the Taft cafeteria, believe it or not, when Rolly Howard, now incarcerated due to the hard work of our assistant, inspector Strange, lit a trash can on fire. This simple event was the moment when I realized my life long calling; to become a high school vice principal. I realized how meaningful it would be to perform mundane tasks and manage irresponsible students in an educational environment and I knew that if I could somehow just put out that fire, it would be a sign that I should continue upon my quest."

By this time everybody was laughing so he stopped and waited for a moment.

"Actually, we did get started the day of the trash can fire, not only through a lot of chance circumstances but also because of Dwight, who somehow saw right from the start that the four of us could work together and do something worthwhile..."

Seth went on to briefly describe how they had worked together to both identify the criminal and apprehend him. Gene pried him on one point, asking, "What did you feel like when the alarm went off in the station last night and the lights came on and Gus jumped out of bed after you Seth?"

"Well... stupid, I guess, is the best description. I'd never even thought of the alarm to tell you the truth or I never would have done it in the first place. I guess it's a pretty dumb way to get a fingerprint-"

Travis interrupted.

"Talk about feeling stupid, how about me flooding the car like a driver's trainee or something?"

"Aw, Travis, you just got a little excited is all. I don't think you were stupid," Greg said supportively.

"Well thanks, Greg. I sure felt stupid at the time."

"Not nearly as stupid as I felt when I finally got control of myself in the car after almost going berserk," Gunther added. Everybody laughed.

Stacy cut into the laughter.

"Well, I'd like to know how you guys got all that information about the criminal. Where did you get all that stuff anyway?" She scrutinized Seth carefully.

"Well, sis, to tell you the truth, we have to keep our sources a secret. Kinda like a reporter. Right Mom?"

"Leave me out of this, young man. I have a reputation to protect and I'd be willing to bet that you fellows went to... extraordinary lengths... to dig up so much information. I'm not surprised that you want to keep it a secret."

There was a glow of pride behind Kelly Knight's stern tone of voice that made her reprimand more of a compliment than anything else. Roxanne finally spoke up.

"You know, I thought it was weird at first that Travis was getting so involved with the newspaper, until the night of the dance and the fire downtown by which point I knew you guys were doing something more than just working on a school newspaper. I just wish that I could have been involved a little. It all sounds so exciting."

"I'd be willing to bet that these guys end up doing all sorts of interesting things together, Roxanne, so if you can tolerate the company long enough you're bound to have a lot of fun with them." Gene said in a thoughtful tone.

Jann Paris just wrapped her arms around Seth's neck and gave him a big squeeze and said,

"I think I'm satisfied knowing it's all over and everyone is safe. If I would have known what you guys were into all this time I would have been worried sick. I don't know how you can stand it, Mr. Knight."

"It's a combination of things, Jann. The main thing is the concept of letting go of your children and allowing them to grow up and be themselves. It's something they're going to do anyway. If you go along with it, you retain them as friends as well as children. The other thing is, I guess I was the same way when I was young."

Kelly interrupted Gene with a loud laugh.

"What do you mean *when* you were young? When haven't you been young, Mr. Troublemaker? You two will always be into something. It's only us women that keep you in line, and that's a fact."

Gene smiled and nodded because it was a fact. A most comfortable fact, too.

CHAPTER TWENTY TWO

"So, you guys, this whole time you've been secretly chasing a serious felon and telling the rest of the world that you were working on the school newspaper. Seth, I feel left out, you know. I thought we were better friends than that. I'm sure I could have helped you somehow-"

"Aw, Dwight, the only one we told anything to was my dad and even he didn't get the whole scoop, man. It was just too much potential trouble for an adult to tangle with. If you knew half of what we had to go through to get where we did-"

"That's another thing, Seth. I can understand not telling the papers everything, but why can't you guys tell me all the juicy details? It's not as though-"

"We promised. We had a long meeting and we promised, Dwight. It really is best that way. Trust me." Seth grinned a big grin.

"Okay, okay. But at least you can tell me what you're going to do with all that reward money. That's a lot of money, you know."

"The reward appears to be growing Dwight. I guess there were a few smaller insurance companies that had offered rewards a few years ago and Hike Strangerson is going to look into it for us. You know, that guy turned out to be pretty cool in his own way. When he found out that our finding Gus wasn't a fluke but was actually a result of teamwork, he called me to apologize and offer congratulations. When he heard that some of the insurance com-

138

panies were trying to back out on paying us he got pretty steamed up. Said they do it all the time and that he knew just how to deal with them. As far as the money goes, I don't think any of us know how we're going to use it, Dwight. Just being finished with this case is a big enough shock in itself. I haven't thought of much else for the last several months. I really can't believe it's all over."

"What about your car, Seth? How are you ever going to replace that?"

A sad look flashed across Seth's face.

"I don't know Dwight. Dad has a friend who has an old mustang in his garage that he never drives so maybe I'll try and buy that car. I don't know. I think that Gus should pay for my car out of his own pocket, but I'd have to get a lawyer to collect on it, so I don't know what to do. Me and Dad will figure it out."

"You think you guys would ever do it again?"

Dwight stared straight into Seth's eyes. There was a long pause as the four boys looked at each other. They all slowly broke into wide grins.

"Absolutely!"

Dwight rubbed his chin thoughtfully and said, "Well, I suppose you'll need a name then. Don't you think?"

There was a long moment of silence. The four boys looked at one another with bewilderment painted all over their faces.

"What do we need a name for?" Seth asked.

Dwight chuckled softly.

"Just as I thought. Without a name, what are you going to put on your business cards when you print them up? What are you going to paint on the doorway of your office when you get one? What are you going to say when you answer the phone in your office? 'Hello, this is Seth. Whaddya want?' "

Seth had a look of amazement on his face. "Wow. I didn't think of that. You're right Dwight. We need a name!"

A discussion began and the four boys began tossing out suggestions, one by one, and laughing and grimacing. Dwight propped his feet up on his desk, watching the boys with a twinkle in his eye. After several rounds of bad ideas Dwight interrupted them.

"I have given this a lot of thought, guys, and I think I've come up with a pretty good idea."

He reached into his top drawer, withdrew a pad of paper and a felt marker and carefully drew something on the pad in large letters.

"I want you to think about it for a minute before you make up your mind."

He held up the pad. It read, **THE SHADOW CLUB**

The four boys looked and pondered, and they all began to nod their heads and look at one another with smiles. Dwight cautiously asked, "So, what do you think?"

Seth responded immediately.

"This sounds great to me Dwight. I'm terrible at naming things, but I think I can recognize something good when I see it and that name is great. I'm already getting an idea for a logo for our business cards!"

They all agreed with him excitedly, and then Dwight smiled and said,

"Just don't forget who your friends are now that you are rich heroes. You know, this group was my idea in the beginning and-"

Greg solemnly interrupted.

"Gee, Dwight, I won't ever forget you. I don't forget nothing."

Everybody laughed, delighted to be in the company of good friends with lots of time ahead to find new adventures to experience together.

Made in the USA
Middletown, DE
31 July 2019